ALL I WANT IS YOU

DJ JAMISON

AUTHOR'S NOTE

The majority of *All I Want Is You* is set in the fictional town of Juniper, Oregon, in the central part of the state. The Northern California city mentioned, Bremer, is also fictional. However, conservative towns do exist in certain areas of both states.

PROLOGUE

"Look," Eli said. "Mistletoe."

He pointed over his head, watched as Turner raised his gaze to the sprig of green, then clumsily lurched forward to press his lips to his best friend's mouth.

It wasn't the smoothest first kiss, but it was amazing — until Turner jerked back a split second later, eyes wide.

"What the *hell*, Eli?" he demanded, looking over his shoulder nervously.

Laughter drifted down the hall. As coach of the track and cross-country teams, Eli's father was hosting the team's holiday party, and the house was full of students. But no one else was in the hallway that led to Eli's bedroom doorway, where he'd taped mistletoe up a couple of hours ago, his heart tripping with fear and excitement.

Eli tried to brazen it out when he saw Turner's reaction. "It's a holiday tradition."

"People could see," Turner said, two blotches of red high on his cheekbones. "Don't you already get enough shit for being gay? Besides, you know I'm not ... into *that*."

Well, now he did. Eli had kind of been hoping Turner *would* be

I

into it. That maybe his gorgeous best friend was harboring a similar desire inside him. Sometimes the way he looked at Eli ...

But no. Eli had been wrong.

Heart aching, he tried to hold his smile. "Sorry. It was just a joke, Turner."

Turner shook his head, eyes narrowed. "Not funny."

No, it wasn't.

Eli had spent months working up the courage to tell Turner how he felt. Each time he tried to say the words, he froze up. This was their senior year, and they'd be going to different universities. Time was running out. Eli had thought the mistletoe plan was a stroke of genius. He would kiss Turner, and if Turner felt the same, he'd know. And if he didn't, he'd be able to blame it on the mistletoe and laugh it off.

But Turner wasn't laughing. He huffed, shaking his head at Eli, and walked away.

Even as the flames of humiliation and shame engulfed him, Eli couldn't help staring after Turner as his broad shoulders turned the corner, his ass sitting high and tight on a pair of long-ass legs that made him a great runner.

God, what if Turner told Eli's dad? He'd been Eli's best friend since preschool, but he was also one of Coach's star runners. A knot formed in Eli's stomach at the thought of what his father might do if he found out. He'd ordered Eli not to act on his *sick urges*.

Coach hadn't been happy when Eli came out, but it'd been a badly kept secret to begin with. Everyone had suspected he was gay. Turns out, suspecting and knowing are two very different things. Now, Eli had no deniability, and neither did Coach.

You've humiliated me and your mother, and if you know what's good for you, you'll shut your mouth about all this gay business and keep it in your pants until you graduate.

Looked like he was on pace to keep it in his pants a good, long time.

Eli retreated to his room to regroup, cycling through stages of mortification and regret. After an hour of listening to emo music and stewing over what happened — and feeling guiltier by the minute for kissing Turner without asking first — Eli returned to the party.

Kids from school drifted through the front rooms, talking and laughing while holding plates of Christmas goodies — fudge, divinity, peanut brittle, chocolate bonbons, banana-nut bread, pumpkin spice cake, and more; his mother had outdone herself as usual — but Eli didn't see Turner.

He worked his way toward the kitchen, not surprised when no one tried to talk to him. His circle of friends had shrunk drastically after he came out. Only the fact he was Coach's son kept the worst bullying in check.

Just when he was about to give up, he spotted Turner standing in the doorway to the enclosed back porch. He stepped forward, intending to apologize. Kara, a pretty blonde standing beside Turner, pointed up. "Look, mistletoe."

Turner laughed and stepped forward, raising a hand to her cheek. Then he kissed her — and the last, tiniest spark of hope in Eli's heart turned to ash.

1

"Eli, you know how you always say you can't visit your family because there's not enough vacation time over Christmas?"

Eli shifted in the uncomfortable chair in front of his supervisor's battered metal desk. The chair had long since worn through any padding for his ass, and the desk looked like it'd seen the wars, if the wars consisted of coffee and Cheetos going to battle.

Rainbow Haven wasn't one of those high-class nonprofits with wealthy donors, though being in California, there were certainly plenty of people with money. It was easy to think of Californians as a liberal, socially minded populace. But this part of northern California was more conservative, and it was still a struggle to get adequate funding for LGBTQ kids in need of shelter or counseling.

"Yeah, the annual Christmas tree auction is our biggest fundraiser, and then there's the planning to do for the year ahead. I don't mind, though."

Barb gave a pained smile. "No, you wouldn't."

She knew all too well that Eli had avoided going home for the four years he'd worked at Rainbow Haven. He'd left home at eighteen and never found a compelling reason to go back.

Juniper, Oregon, wasn't a happy place for a gay teenager, and he seriously doubted it was any better for a sexually active gay man. Not that he'd been terribly active lately. The club scene wasn't his forte. Everywhere he turned, there were young guys with far more sparkle. He had trouble seeing why anyone would choose him: slim, brunet, and bland, over one of those toned, twinkling twinks. God, he was only twenty-six, and they made him feel old.

"Barb, what's up?" he asked. "Do you need me to step in as Santa? I might need a bonus," he joked.

"Even better," she said with mock cheer. "You can go home and see your family!"

Eli didn't have a good feeling about this. "I can?"

"And take as much time as you like. Reconnect with your family, and ... and ..."

Her eyes filled with tears. Oh, fuck.

Eli gripped the arms of his chair tightly. "They cut my position, didn't they?"

By "they" he meant the board of directors. They ultimately made the tough funding decisions.

When you work in the nonprofit sector, funding is always an issue. There's not really such a thing as job security. But Eli had been in his position as marketing and events coordinator for the Rainbow Haven youth shelter long enough that he'd gotten comfortable and forgotten that little fact.

Barb shook her head no, but just as relief swept him, her next words crashed over him. "They're closing us down."

He gaped at her, horrified.

"The entire shelter? But the kids ..."

She pushed her fingertips to the corners of her eyes, absorbing the tears. Then, taking a deep breath, she gave him a sad smile, but a more genuine one. "It's not all bad. They're merging with Pride Place. Together, the budgets will allow for a new, larger shelter."

"Oh... good," he said. "That's good."

Eli was relieved that the teens outcast and shunned for their sexuality, even worse than he had been, would have the help they needed. But now that he knew they'd be taken care of, his own situation came to the forefront of his mind.

"Oh, shit."

"I'm sorry," Barb said. "I tried to save your job, but Pride Place has an entire marketing department."

Eli nodded numbly. "Makes sense."

Barb said tentatively, "Maybe this is an opportunity, though? For you and your family?"

Eli hadn't been home since he left for college. He'd always justified it in his mind by telling himself he had to work or to save the expense of travel. But deep down, he knew he was just making excuses. Truth was, he just didn't want to face his father's disapproval again.

Now, though, Eli had no good reason to stay away.

Fuck. He had *no job*.

"I have to go home, don't I?" he said with a sigh.

Barb, who was a friend as much as she was his boss, nodded. "I think it's probably time. You can take the holidays to find some peace before you launch the job hunt."

Oh, Jesus. The job hunt. That would be horrendous. Jobs like this one didn't grow on trees, as Eli's father loved to say as Eli was growing up.

Oh, Jesus. His father. Eli would have to see him again.

Or he could stay in California. Alone and jobless. On Christmas.

"Uh-uh," Barb said. Over the years, she'd come to know Eli too well. "You need to stop avoiding this, Eli, and now you have the perfect opportunity."

Eli scoffed. "Oh, sure. 'Hey, Mom and Dad, I'm back. I'm so successful I've turned up with no job! I'm alone and miserable too, just like you warned me I'd be. No, I haven't been to church lately.'"

Barb let him get the dramatics out of his system, then calmly pointed out the one little detail that would make him cave. "There was the card."

Eli groaned. The fucking birthday card. Eli's father had written in it, "We miss you and love you. Always."

Barb and Eli had analyzed that card to death. Had his dad softened his stance? Would he be open to having a gay son now? Had time and distance dulled his disappointment? And if it had, was Eli ready to forgive his father if it meant having a family again?

All good questions — ones he couldn't begin to answer unless he went home.

And then there was Turner ...

He'd never told Barb about him. It was too cliché: the gay kid falling in unrequited love with his best friend. No doubt, Turner had moved on from Juniper. He could very well be married by now.

Eli's chest tightened, and he took a deep breath. He didn't miss Turner. You didn't miss someone after eight years. You moved on. You took an occasional stroll down memory lane and looked at photos when you wanted to prod at old wounds, and then you went out and found a guy to date or fuck, depending on whether you were delusional enough to believe you could be boyfriend material.

Eli wasn't. Never had been. He was basically a disaster on all fronts.

His job was the one good thing he had going for him. And now it was gone.

Eli spared a thought for Barb now that the shock had worn off. "What about you? Your job..."

"They're keeping me on," Barb said, sounding guilty. "I tried to fight for you. They said maybe in the future, if they have something open up ..."

"I get it." Eli dredged up a smile. "I'm glad you'll be okay."

"You will too," she said. "You're like a cat. You always land on your feet."

Must be true. His dad had always hated cats.

December 12th

A five-hour drive, two gut-bomb burgers, and enough soda to float him down the Klamath River later, Eli passed the Welcome to Juniper sign. Snowflakes whirled over his windshield, adding to the accumulation on the roads.

The snow didn't surprise him. Juniper was in Central Oregon on the east side of the Cascade Mountains, and it wasn't unusual to get a few inches each year. But it didn't do much for Eli's frayed nerves. After so long living in California, he was ill-equipped to drive in snowy conditions.

He tightened his grip on the wheel, and focused on the street ahead, but his gaze kept getting drawn to the familiar sights, which knotted his stomach with just as much anxiety as the shitty weather did.

Some memories were more pleasant than others.

The elementary school brought a rush of fond nostalgia, with the teeter-totters that Eli and Turner had treated with little to no caution, jumping off to let the other boy slam into the ground or attempting to ride it while standing up. Boy stuff that would send today's educators into heart palpitations, no doubt, but which had been accepted when they were kids as boys being boys. He grinned as he passed the swings, remembering the time Turner sprained an ankle in fourth grade from jumping out while sky high. Eli had chickened out and jumped from a lower height. Turner had limped for a week, but he'd gotten all the glory too, and that had just been the beginning of the turning point. Turner became the athlete, while Eli retreated into books, movies, and PlayStation games. Their friendship had held strong, despite their differences, until Eli's pathetic teenage heart ruined everything.

A few blocks later, Eli passed a row of houses decked out with inflated snowmen and reindeer pulling Santa. The high school loomed ahead, its long football field with artificial turf still a bright green even in winter. That sight made Eli's chest tighten. There was no happy nostalgia now. Instead, Eli remembered the cruel taunts he'd endured the last year and a half there. He'd never been bashed, not when the track coach was his father and his best friend was a popular athlete. But he'd still been hurt.

Turner had his back, though. Even when it wasn't fun to be his friend, he'd stuck with Eli. Even after that humiliating moment under the mistletoe, he'd shown up at school after winter break and fallen into step beside Eli as if nothing had happened. But everything had changed. Turner had a new girlfriend, and Eli had tried and failed not to feel the jealousy that seared his insides whenever he saw them together. He'd pulled away, bit by bit, until they were barely acquaintances who nodded in the halls.

Eli didn't spot the stop sign until he was on top of it. He stupidly slammed the brakes, which sent him sliding into the intersection. He yanked the wheel, turning right, so he'd only cross one lane of traffic rather than two. The car fishtailed, and he cursed his luck. Owning a banana-yellow convertible Camaro had been fun in California, but in a snowy Oregon? Not so much.

Eli turned into the skid, remembering that much, and managed to bring the car under control, wincing as a horn blared behind him. He took the next turn, getting his dumb ass off the busier street. Juniper was small, thankfully, so he was able to easily navigate to his parents' house six blocks away via quieter side streets. They, too, were packed with snow, but with no other traffic, he drove without incident, taking in the strings of Christmas lights beginning to flicker on one by one under the dreary, darkening afternoon sky.

His parents' neighborhood had a tradition of putting out handmade Christmas cards crafted from plywood and lights — and any other supplies they chose to decorate with, and there were *many* variations. Eli could still remember reluctantly helping his father assemble a new one each year — it wasn't enough to make one and recycle it; they had to make a new one year after year. His dad had been obsessed with outdoing the neighbors, and Eli had dreaded the experience, which inevitably ended in cursing and his father's annoyance with his failure to be of any help.

As Eli pulled into the driveway, the Miller residence card blinked on and off, with red and green lights that spelled out "Merry Xmas." On the other side, the Kemmers' giant plywood card was painted a deep green and lined with silvery tinsel. Cutout stencil letters backed by a spotlight spelled out "Joy to the World."

But Eli's childhood home stood dark and lonely.

For one moment, Eli's gut clenched with fear. *What if they weren't there?*

Then he spotted a light in the window at the far corner of the house, and reason returned. They were still here, in the place he'd left them.

Now, he just had to get out of the car and face them.

———

A bright yellow Camaro fishtailed as it took the corner in front of them with inches to spare.

"I'm sorry, Mr. T!" Michael exclaimed, hands so tight on the steering wheel his knuckles turned white. "He came out of nowhere!" He faltered. "Didn't he? Fuck, I need my license!"

"Language," Turner said calmly, even as his heart hammered. That had been a close call. The asshole Camaro driver should have yielded, but he wasn't surprised that the owner of a douchey car would be a douche. "It wasn't your fault."

Turner jotted down what he could remember of the tag number. California plates. Obviously, some asshole who didn't know how to drive in bad weather.

"So, I'm not getting docked, right?" Michael asked nervously. "This is the driving test, so…"

Turner sighed. Michael wasn't the most confident driver, but he'd squeak by. "Not this time. Take it as a life lesson, guys," he said, addressing the two other students in the back seat, as well. "Defensive driving means being ready for drivers like that. Plus, having snow on the ground turns some people into fools. They stomp the brake instead of easing into it. Or they lose control and slide right into another lane."

He nodded toward the next corner. "Let's head back to the school."

Michael parked crookedly, but within the lines, and Turner handed him the slip that he could take to the DMV to get a license.

"Thanks, T!"

"That's Mr. T to you," Turner said sternly, and Michael laughed. Coach Harp had shown the track and cross-country teams an old "A-Team" episode, and ever since, Turner had been Mr. T. He was pretty sure Coach just hadn't wanted to share his title, even with an assistant coach, but Turner didn't mind the nickname.

Behind them, Dakota Redding grumbled. "Too bad I'm not on the cross-country team. No way the coach would overlook *me* nearly rear-ending a car."

Turner sighed and stuck his pen behind his ear, striding toward the entrance.

"Hurry it up, girls. The bell will ring soon." He cast a look at Dakota. "You're up next class for your final driving exam. Make sure you practice checking your blind spot."

"I always check," she said. "You just don't see me checking because you're looking over your shoulder."

He tipped his head toward the building, expression neutral. "See you next week."

The last week before winter break, thank fuck. The coaches at Juniper High typically got stuck with one of two classes: driver's ed or physical education. In some ways, he was happier with driver's ed because the students wanted to be there, but it could also be hell on his nerves.

So, maybe Dakota had a point that he was watching the road more than her, but he sure as hell could not trust these kids enough to put his life totally into their hands. He watched for traffic so that incidents like today's didn't end in accidents. He couldn't think of a quicker way to lose his job.

"Hey, Mr. T!" a long-legged redhead called as she passed by in the hall. Rachelle was one of the team's fastest distance runners, and he'd been coaching her for nearly her entire high school career. "You gonna play Santa at the party next weekend?"

Every year, Coach Harp donned the big, red suit and played Santa. Turner was the lucky man who got to carry out all those traditions as Coach recovered from surgery.

"Ho-ho-ho," he said dryly.

She laughed. "I can't wait to see that."

Then she was gone, catching up with her friends. Turner shook his head, making a mental note to ask Mrs. Harp for the suit so he could get it dry-cleaned before the following weekend. The things he did for Coach and his team.

Eli parked the car and had only just stepped out when the front door flew open.

"Eli," his mother called, hurtling down the stairs with a speed that worried him. She flew into his arms, smothering him in a hug. "You're back."

"For Christmas," he said faintly.

"Your father will be so happy to see you," his mom said, loosening the stranglehold she had on him.

"You're sure?" Eli asked, anxiety a steady weight in his chest now. He didn't feel ready to face his father again, but he could hardly turn around and drive back to California at this hour.

His mom smiled through the tears. "Yes," she said emphatically. "He's regretted his words to you for so long, Eli. I've told you this."

So she had. He hadn't believed her then, and he was skeptical now. He'd find out soon enough.

"You're not mad I've gone so long without a visit?"

She laughed. "Oh, I'm mad all right," she said. "You're in a lot of trouble. We'll save the lecture for after I get a hot bowl of venison stew in you."

He groaned as his mouth immediately watered. His stomach didn't need more in it, but his memory of her perfectly spiced stew disagreed. Eli grabbed his bags and followed her into the warmth of his childhood home.

"Your father's resting," she said, "but he'll be up and about soon. His hours have been out of whack, and the pain pills make him drowsy."

"Pain pills?" Eli echoed.

She paused, gesturing down the hall. "Your dad had knee replacement surgery. Nothing life-threatening, but it's been hard."

The living room had been updated with new cream-colored carpet and a pale blue sofa accented with pink and gray throw pillows. It gave the room a lighter feel than he remembered, but it wasn't entirely changed. His father's leather La-Z Boy recliner still sat in the corner, complete with ash burns from the cigars he smoked. Come to think of it, though, the house was clear of the sweet, smoky scent the cigars usually left in their wake.

"The house looks nice…"

"Oh, thanks," his mother said, distractedly as she dug through a drawer in the cherrywood desk in the corner where his parents had always managed their bills with a frown of concentration and a large calculator. Now, at least, Eli saw they'd added a laptop. Hopefully that meant they'd moved into online banking and the twenty-first century at last.

"Does Coach still smoke cigars?"

"Hmm?" She rifled through drawers, and Eli adjusted his grip on his duffel bags, which he hadn't yet put down — a subconscious reluctance to commit to staying, perhaps? — and crossed the room to her.

"I asked if Coach still smoked. What are you doing?"

"Oh, he gave up smoking, thank heavens. Principal Riggs died of lung cancer, poor man. It really shook your father. He quit cold turkey."

She turned, holding out a garage door opener. "Here it is! So you can park in the garage. You don't want that little car to freeze overnight. This weather is just awful."

"Thanks."

"You can move it after you get settled. Your room is still there for you. I haven't redecorated, but you've been gone so long it's become a bit of an extra storage space. Sorry about that."

"It's been a long time, Mom. You didn't have to keep my room for me."

She blinked at him. "Of course I did. You're my baby boy. Just because you gave up on us doesn't mean we gave up on you."

"So much for feeding me before the lecture," he said lightly.

"No, no," she said, pasting on a smile. "Go put your bags away and freshen up. It's early still, but the stew has been simmering all day. I'll dish you up some whenever you're ready."

"Then the lecture?" he asked.

"With a side of guilt trip," she promised, but he could tell from her warm eyes that she was only teasing.

She wasn't kidding about his room. He walked in to see that his posters of a younger Chris Evans still held pride of place on the wall next to his bed. The room looked just as he'd left it, except for the collection of about a dozen plastic storage tubs taking up floor space.

His old dresser, made of a pale pinewood, stood against the opposite wall.

Dropping his bags onto the bed, he turned to check, and yep, the second drawer still had the gouge from when he and Turner had been roughhousing and he'd fallen against the dresser with a spoon in his hand. Turns out mock sword-fighting with silverware in a small space isn't a good idea. Who knew?

On impulse, he pulled the dresser out from the wall and squatted down to look at the secret message he'd carved on the back — a way to express something he could tell absolutely no one at the time. E+T inside a crudely drawn heart. He remembered his heart pounding as he made the carving with a small pocket knife his grandfather had given him, crafting potential lies he could use if anyone ever discovered it. The T could stand for Teresa, a pretty blond girl one grade above him. There were a lot of T names. It didn't *have* to mean Turner.

Eli ran the pad of his finger over the etching, the lines rough against his softer skin. "Welcome home," he murmured.

"Eli?" a deep voice called, and Eli lurched to his feet, heart hammering. Just as he might have done when he was sixteen, he panicked and shoved the dresser with its forbidden love note back against the wall. "You here, son?"

His father was calling. And there was no more avoiding his past.

2

E li had never seen his father cry before. Not even when he'd gone to his grandmother's funeral. Coach Harp had sat stoic, empty-eyed with grief, but dry-eyed too. Eli's dad had always been a tough asshole who believed men should live and breathe sports and cars and drinking beer. Eli only enjoyed one of those three — and it wasn't sports, to his father's great disappointment.

But Coach's eyes were wet now as Eli hesitated in the doorway.

"Saw you go by in the hall," he said in a hoarse voice. "Thought the damn pills were making me hallucinate."

Coach struggled to get up, and Eli stepped inside the dark bedroom. He was tied up in knots over talking to his father, but more than that, he was concerned Coach was going to hurt himself.

"Don't get up," Eli said. "Your knee—"

"Is a damn pain in the ass."

Eli snorted. "Don't you mean it's a pain in the knee?"

A pained smile touched Coach's mouth. "That too."

That explained the tears, maybe. A knee replacement was routine, but from what Eli had heard, it wasn't painless.

"Do you need pain pills? Or ice?" Eli asked, clueless about his father's care.

His dad waved a hand and sank back against his pillows. He looked older than Eli remembered. Eight years had gone by, sure, but his mom essentially looked the same. Maybe she had a few more crinkles around her eyes, and she clearly dyed her hair, but she was the mom he remembered. But Coach looked *old*. His face sagged as he shifted, groaning with discomfort.

"I can't believe you're really here," Coach said raggedly when he'd given up making himself comfortable.

Eli took a step toward the bed, hovering over his dad awkwardly. "Yeah. For the holidays. You know."

"It's been so long. Thought I might never see you again." His voice cracked, and Eli looked into his father's eyes, startled to see more of those tears. He felt an ache in his own chest in response. He didn't feel sorry for his father, but he understood the feeling. He hadn't been sure he'd ever be welcome at home again.

The heartache was balanced by anger. Long-simmering anger that had been bottled up for too long.

"Sure you want me here? I'm still a faggot." He made sure his voice dripped as much venom as his father's had all those years ago. "I won't hide it, and anyone who doesn't like it can go to hell. That includes you."

Coach grimaced and scrubbed a hand down his face before answering. "Christ, Eli, it's the holidays. Can't we just get along?"

"I guess that's up to you," Eli said. "I'm still gay, so if that's a deal-breaker, I'll grab my bags and go."

"It's not a deal-breaker."

"So you accept me?"

"Yes."

"In theory or in practice?"

His father squinted. "I don't even know what the hell that means."

"It means, *Coach*, that it's one thing to accept your son is gay and another to welcome his boyfriend home with him for the holidays, or to go to his wedding—"

"You're getting *married?*"

"Not yet," Eli said impatiently. Probably not anytime soon, if ever. But he had a point to make, and his shitty record with men wasn't going to stop him.

Coach glanced to the doorway behind him and cleared his throat. "So, uh, is there a boyfriend here with you?" His eyes shot back to Eli. "It's okay either way, Eli. I just want my son back."

His father was trying, which was more than Eli had ever dared to imagine, so he held back the words on the tip of his tongue. *You once said I wasn't your son anymore. You once said I could go to hell alone and miserable if I wanted a perverted lifestyle.*

"No boyfriend," Eli said, relenting. "Just me."

"Okay, then," his father said uncertainly. "I'm glad you're here. We're okay, aren't we? You'll stay?"

Eli hadn't forgotten his father's words, and he hadn't forgiven him for the homophobia that drove Eli away. But he was tired, hungry, and too emotionally drained to continue the conversation.

"I'll stay for now," he said. "Mom's got venison stew on the stove. Hard to resist that."

"Well, hot damn, don't let me keep you," his dad said. "You've got to be dying to get a taste after so long."

Eli chuckled. "I did miss Mom's cooking."

"Try to leave enough for your old man," Coach said. "I can't take another pill on an empty stomach."

Eli's mother stepped into the room, a steaming bowl in one hand. "I've got some for you right here since you missed lunch," she said. "I was just waiting for you to wake up." She glanced at Eli. "The pills make him drowsy, so he's been sleeping at all hours. But soon he'll start physical therapy and cut back on the dosage."

"Don't talk about me like I'm not in the room," Coach groused.

As his mother fussed over Coach, setting his bowl of soup on a bedside table and smoothing his blankets, Eli headed for the doorway. "I'm gonna grab myself some."

"Eli," his dad called as he reached the door.

"Yeah?"

"I really am glad you're home. What I said back then ... Those were different times."

It wasn't an apology. Then again, he wasn't sure he'd ever heard Coach apologize for anything. It was probably the closest he'd ever get to one. Eli didn't know yet if it was enough to begin healing the wounds Coach inflicted when Eli was a teenager.

Only time would tell.

Turner was inputting grades from the final written exam in his four driver's education classes when his phone rang. He checked the time on his computer as he picked up the phone, wincing to see it was already going on 6 p.m. He'd been so engrossed in the tedious data entry that he'd lost all track of time. Scout would be fit to be tied when he got home.

The cellphone ID indicated it was his mother. "Hey, Mom."

"Turner, I was just thinking about Christmas. Maybe I should make something to take to the Harps' place? Molly's been so great, and I know she loves to bake, but Coach just had that surgery, and I worry it's too much for her to cater to us."

His mother spoke quickly, her voice filled with an anxiety that never used to be there. Ever since Turner's father died, she walked around as if she didn't trust the earth under her feet.

Not that her world was the only one shaken by Hal Williams' death. Turner was in his senior year at Oregon State when it happened, and he'd scrapped his plans to pursue a career in university athletics to return home. He was just lucky Coach had talked the Juniper school administration into adding an assistant coach position on the condition he had a teaching certificate and picked up some classes, as well. A small town like Juniper only had so many jobs. It helped that the school's track and cross-country program was one of the best in the state and that Coach had presented it as an opportunity to groom the next head coach for when he retired.

"I'm sure Molly would appreciate anything you wanted to bring," Turner said carefully. His mother had never been exceptional in the kitchen, but he didn't want to hurt her feelings. "Maybe you could buy a nice wine or make those cute pinwheels with the cream cheese. Those are good."

"You think that's enough?"

"Mom, I've been going by a few times a week to check on Coach and Molly. They're doing fine, and by Christmas Day, I expect Coach will be on his feet again. But how about this? I'll ask her."

"When?"

Turner sighed, pinching the bridge of his nose. He was tired, and a headache was forming behind his eyes, but he knew his mother well enough to know she'd only work herself up more if he didn't promise to do it soon.

"How about first thing tomorrow morning?" he suggested.

"Thanks, honey," she said, her voice a fraction less stressed. "You're such a good boy to look out for them."

Lately, it seemed like Turner looked out for everyone. Not that he minded. He loved the Harps. He hadn't always loved Coach Harp — he could be a tough man to like at times, much less love — but the way he and Molly had stepped up to support them when his father died had done a lot to soothe his ragged edges over Coach's treatment of Eli. He'd never really forgive Coach for chasing off his son, but Turner figured he probably shared in the blame. If he'd been brave enough to come out as bisexual back then — or at least return Eli's kiss without freaking out — Eli might have realized he didn't need to push everyone away and hide from his life in Juniper.

Running errands for his mom, who stayed in the house more and more these days, helping his divorced sister with two busy kids, and keeping up with the maintenance on three homes took its toll. Turner was tired. And, hell, keeping busy was good, but it wasn't a cure for loneliness.

Turner wanted a family of his own. So far, it was just him and Scout, but he still held out hope it wouldn't always be just the two of them.

"Knock-knock."

Turner looked up to see his fifteen-year-old niece standing in the doorway. She wore tights, a red sweater dress, and her blue-streaked blonde hair was pulled up into a messy bun. On her ears, two reindeer heads with ruby-red noses dangled, a gruesome bit of holiday jewelry, if you asked Turner. Which Cassie never did.

"Hey," she said. "You going home soon? I could use a ride."

Turner glanced at his computer display. He'd nearly finished inputting test scores and could easily do the rest during his planning period the next day. He'd missed his evening run because of the weather, so he'd worked ahead. Now, his body hummed with latent energy that had nowhere to go.

"Sure. Give me a minute to pack up."

As he shoved the tests into a drawer and locked it, his niece slumped into the chair in front of him. "I can't wait until winter break. Amelia is kicking our asses—"

Turner cleared his throat meaningfully.

"—our butts," Cassie immediately corrected. "I don't even have a lead part, and she has me running through my lines over and over."

"Which ghost are you again?"

"Christmas Future."

"The best one," Turner said, tousling her hair on the way to the door. "They gonna let you keep your blue streaks?"

"Yes," she said, a hint of annoyance in her voice. "I'm from the future. Maybe everyone dyed their hair."

Turner paused in the hallway to lock his office door. "Wait a minute. Doesn't that ghost dress like a reaper? You have a hood, don't you?"

"That's beside the point," Cassie said loftily.

Turner smirked. "Right."

He'd been giving her a hard time about her hair since she started streaking it, but it was all in fun. She made fun of his beard and T-shirt-and-jeans fashion sense, calling him boring, and he teased her about her latest fashion choices, which seemed to change every two months.

"You gonna let me drive?" she asked on the way to his army green Jeep Wrangler, parked in the faculty parking lot.

"Nope."

"Because of the weather?"

"Because you're fifteen."

"Old enough for a learner's permit."

Turner paused by the Jeep. "Do you have a permit?"

"No," she said. "It's not fair. You're the driver's ed teacher! You could let me drive under your supervision, right?"

"Not outside of driver's ed," he said. "And we only accept students who are old enough to get a license. You know that."

Cassie stuck out her lip. "Having an uncle who teaches driving should get me some sort of advantage."

"It gets you a ride home after six," he said. "Get in."

Cassie gave in and climbed into the passenger side with a huff. Turner started the engine and let Cassie stew for half the drive before saying, "I could teach you to drive, if your mom says it's okay." Cassie started to squeal, and he had to raise his voice to be heard. "But not in this weather. Talk to me in the spring."

Cassie bounced in her seat. "Thank you, thank you, thank you, Uncle Turner! You're the best!"

Turner wasn't so sure about that. He kind of thought he was a schmuck who let fifteen-year-old girls manipulate him. But he just smiled and drove away before he could get wrangled into any more ill-begotten plans.

It was past time to get home to Scout.

3

December 13th

Eli woke early, the smell of coffee and bacon seeping into troubled dreams of wandering the halls of Juniper High — dressed, thankfully, but with students demanding to know why he'd come back where he wasn't wanted. Two football players had loomed over him, as if he were a child, rather than a slender man of their height or even the gangly teen he had been. "Coach Harp isn't here to protect you," one had snarled.

"Yeah, he doesn't have to pretend he's not disgusted by his own son," another said.

Then his stomach had growled, and the scene had melted away as he blinked his eyes open. Coffee. Bacon. The faint sizzle and clatter of his mother in the kitchen.

Welcome to Juniper, he thought wryly. *Let's hope reality is kinder than your own messed-up dreams.*

It was no wonder he'd been restless the night before and that all his fears had invaded when he did manage to sleep. It had been a strained evening despite Coach "accepting" Eli as he was. It felt like an uneasy truce rather than true peace, with Eli's mother working overtime to serve as a bridge between them.

With a gusty exhale, he got up and walked into the hall dressed in boxers and a tank top.

His mother kept the house too warm most of the time, and it was made even worse by her nonstop baking as Christmas approached. But it wouldn't feel like Christmas without her sugar cookies, spice cakes, and pies covering every surface. He'd been gone a long time, but it only just now hit him how much he'd missed the traditions he grew up with. He could have made his own pies — he was a functioning adult and had been cooking for himself for years — but he'd known it wouldn't be the same. Instead, he'd gone to parties with friends and tried to pretend he didn't miss the scent of flour and nutmeg drifting through his house. Not to mention the over-the-top decorations. It was a wonder his parents hadn't set up a Christmas tree yet, but then they'd been preoccupied with Coach's surgery. That hadn't stopped his mother from covering every surface in holiday statuettes, from Santas, to snowmen, to reindeer. Her absolute favorite figurines were angels. She had a whole collection of them standing watch over the fireplace, where eight stockings were lined up.

That was different. Eli drifted over to check out the names painstakingly handstitched across the top of each stocking.

Coach. Molly. Elijah.

Turner.

Eli's belly swooped. Turner had his own family, and he'd always spent holidays with them. Eli read over the rest the names, his confusion growing.

Daisy. That was Turner's mother. Krystal. His older sister. Cassie and Anthony. Turner's niece and nephew. Why would they have stockings here? And Eli couldn't help but notice there was one conspicuous name not included: Hal Williams, Turner's father.

Did Turner's parents divorce? What about his sister's husband? Did he leave too? The alternative didn't bear thinking about.

"Mom," he called, turning from the stockings.

"In the kitchen!"

Right. The delicious aromas of bacon and coffee curled around him once more as he went to her. She beamed a smile at him. "How many pancakes do you want? I already plated up some bacon and eggs."

Eli looked at the heaping helping she'd already given him. "Uh, just one. What I really want is coffee."

"Help yourself," she said, going back to humming a Christmas tune quietly as she worked.

Eli took down a mug and poured coffee from the carafe freshly brewed. "Why does Turner have a stocking here? And all of his family?"

His mother's happy humming faltered. "Well, honey, we've had Christmas with them for a few years now."

"Oh."

She turned down the burners and turned to face him. "Turner's father died, and Daisy was a wreck when it happened. It was all rather sudden. To think of that happening to your father..." She placed a hand over her heart. "She was devastated."

"Yeah, of course. I didn't know."

His mother nodded. "Maybe I should have told you, but you were happy, and I didn't see the sense in it. There was enough sadness. Why spread it any farther?"

"I understand," Eli said. He'd felt so far removed from Juniper — and from Turner — that he wasn't sure how he would have felt. Would he have returned for the funeral? Maybe. Probably. Despite the distance that had grown between him and Turner, they'd been friends for their whole childhood. In a lot of ways, they were like brothers, except Eli could never bring himself to think of Turner in a platonic manner. A big part of the reason he hadn't kept in touch with him.

No one needs an unrequited gay friend with a hard-on. Turner had moved on to girlfriends, and Eli wouldn't have been able to do anything but obsess over Turner's relationships if he'd stayed in touch. Sometime during college, while Turner was dating a curvy redhead, Eli unfriended him so he wouldn't have to see his happy, traditional life play out.

He'd missed his friend, but he hadn't missed the crushing jealousy.

Eli swallowed. "So, does that mean Turner will be here on Christmas? With his family?"

"Well, yes, Eli. Turner has never—"

The sound of the front door cut her short. She paused, tilting her head, then smiled. "Well, you'll see."

Turner pulled into Coach's driveway, tires crunching over snow. A set of tire tracks to his right had him wondering if Molly had ventured out into the weather despite his offers to help. Surely Coach was in no shape to drive yet.

Unfolding his long, six-foot-three frame from his Jeep, he promptly sank into the snow, wetting the bottoms of his running tights. He'd already taken his eager border collie out on their regular morning run, making a five-mile loop that had been mostly cleared of snow in city limits. Their preferred running trail in a more wooded area would have to wait another day or two.

Scout had woken Turner with dramatic whines and whimpers, anxious to get out after having to make do with a measly backyard romp the night before. Turner often took Scout out during track and cross-country practices and let him keep pace with the kids, but they were in a lull between seasons at the moment, and the weather and work had prevented Turner from taking him for a proper jog.

Considering he loved running as much as his dog, he hadn't

been happy either. Running could be a bit of an addiction for Turner. Taking Scout along kept him from overdoing it — as he had before, to his body's detriment — because he was convinced his dog would run until he dropped if Turner let him.

He opened the passenger-side door, and Scout jumped out, yipping happily as he dipped his snout down and flung snow into the air. Turner paused only briefly to smile at his happy dog. The wet snow was seeping through his running shoes to dampen his socks, so he hurried toward the porch. He'd have to borrow some snow boots and shovel the drive while he was here. It would probably make him late to pick up Cassie and get to school, but just imagining Coach attempting to go outside and falling made him cringe.

Coach was a tough son of a gun, but only a week out from a knee replacement surgery, he was fragile too.

Scout passed him, turning at the front door to look back impatiently as Turner chose his steps carefully, having no desire to slip and fall on his ass. Turner didn't bother to knock. He'd been popping in every couple of days to run errands and help Molly with her cantankerous patient, and even before then, he'd spent most of his childhood treating the Harps' place like a second home.

He grabbed Scout's collar, keeping him from tracking snow all over the carpets, and used a small towel Molly kept by the door to wipe Scout's paws and underbelly before setting him loose. Shedding his own wet shoes, he headed into the house.

"Hello, sweetie! Did you come over just to beg? Oh, those sad, puppy eyes ..." Molly's voice drifted from the kitchen, along with the sound of low male laughter. Coach must be up early today.

Turner could smell bacon and coffee, and his stomach growled, insisting the granola bar he'd had that morning wasn't enough.

"Morning, Molly," he called. "Do you guys have some salt to put down out there? I can shovel the drive before I—"

His words dried up in his mouth. Molly wasn't alone. She turned from the sizzling pan with a wide smile.

"Turner, look who's here!"

Turner was looking. He couldn't stop looking.

Eli, dressed in boxer shorts and a tank top that was indecently tight for family breakfast, looked up from where he'd crouched down to rub Scout's ears. His green eyes were just as bright as Turner remembered beneath his dark brown hair.

"Turner," he said, his voice a warm tenor, "what are you doing here?"

Turner, still thrown by Eli's sudden appearance, responded with an edge to his voice. "That's a funny question coming from you."

Turner wanted to call the words back as soon as they were out. Eight years apart — five with no contact at all — and that's what he said? He had so many things he wanted to say, that he'd thought about over the years, but they piled up behind the emotion clogging his throat.

"Turner's been helping us since your dad's surgery," Molly said. "He coaches at the school, just like Dad."

Turner wouldn't say *just like* Bill Harp. He'd say a damn sight differently, not that he'd contradict Molly. The Harps had been very good to his family, and he respected them both, even if he didn't always agree with Coach's tough love approach to his job. Or his son, for that matter. But Turner knew that he was at least partially to blame for Eli's disappearing act. He hadn't given Eli a reason to come home, had he? One kiss so brief it might not have happened, and Turner had decimated their friendship by rejecting Eli and turning to the first girl who showed an interest.

Eli gave Scout one last pat to the head and straightened up. He was still slim, but he'd grown into his body in the years since Turner had seen him. He'd lost the gangly, awkward limbs and transitioned into tawny. Svelte. One of those ridiculous adjectives that meant hot as hell.

"Well, I'm here now. I can take care of things."

"I don't mind helping out," Turner said, dropping a hand to Scout's head when he returned to his side, possibly sensing the tension growing in the room.

"Maybe I mind."

"Oh, honey, don't," Molly said, casting an apologetic look Turner's way. "Turner's been so good to us."

Eli didn't look at her. He hadn't looked away from Turner once since he'd walked in.

"Sorry," Eli said, nibbling at his bottom lip. Turner only realized in that moment that Eli was nervous, not angry. "I didn't mean to sound like a dick."

"Eli, language," his mother said.

Turner's lips twitched as Eli corrected course. "A jerk. I only got in yesterday, and I'm cranky until at least my third cup of coffee."

"It's fine." Turner had been the one to initiate hostility after all. He couldn't blame Eli for responding in kind.

"I just meant that you probably have better things to do than run errands for my parents."

Turner looked him square in the eye. "We're all like family. We help each other. You've been gone a long time, so maybe you forgot that."

Eli flushed, and goddamn he was pretty with his cheeks glowing pink. "Guess so." He rebounded. "But I'm here now, so ..."

Molly slid the last of the bacon onto a plate and set it on the table. "Are you staying for breakfast, Turner?"

Turner eyed the bacon, then Eli.

Tempting.

"Nah. I better get going," he said. "I'm all sweaty from my run. I've got to shower and pick up Cassie."

"You ran in this weather?" Molly asked, aghast.

Turner flashed a smile at Molly. "I run every day if I can, rain or shine—"

"Or snow," Eli added.

"Some fool might have slid into you, and then where'd you be?" she said, looking concerned.

"In the hospital, I imagine," Eli said.

Molly fluttered her hands. "Don't even say it!"

"I'm always careful," Turner said, glaring at Eli. What the hell was he thinking worrying his mother like that? And why was he suddenly back after all this time, walking around in his underwear like he lived here?

In the house he grew up in. His family home, not yours. Get a grip, Turner.

"Eli's visiting for Christmas vacation. He's here until New Year's," Molly said brightly. "Isn't that great?"

"Yeah," Turner echoed. "Great."

Eli's didn't say anything, biting into a piece of bacon. Scout quickly became his best friend, butting his head up against Eli's bare knee. "Can I give Hooch some of the bacon?"

"That's not Hooch."

Eli glanced down with a frown. "Oh."

"This beggar is Scout. He's been with me two years."

"I'm sorry," Eli said. "And about your father. Mom just told me this morning."

Turner nodded sharply. "Things happen. Life goes on."

Eli met his eyes. "Yeah, I guess it does."

"But sure, give Scout a nibble if you want. Then I better be going."

Eli broke off a piece of bacon, and Scout gulped it from his fingers, then licked them for good measure. Eli grinned, glancing up at Turner. "I think Scout and I are going to be very good friends."

Eli was gorgeous with his morning stubble and tousled hair, and the sight of that smile made Turner's breath catch. He felt his heart speed up, and internally cursed himself. Was he really that easy? Eli disappears for nearly a decade, and thirty seconds in his presence reduces Turner to mush?

Annoyed with himself, he turned on his heel. "Don't forget to shovel the drive," he said. "Come on, Scout. Time to go."

It wasn't until Turner was on his way to pick up Cassie, freshly showered and shaved for school, that he realized he'd never asked Molly about how she wanted to handle Christmas Day.

Eli was still reeling from seeing Turner again when Coach came into the room, shuffling along with the help of a walker. Seeing his father look so old and frail was a shock to the system, but it didn't last long as his father's booming voice rang out, strong as ever.

"I hate this fucking thing," he said. "Makes me look like I'm ready for the nursing home."

Eli bit his lip and looked away, unable to disagree. It was enlightening, seeing his father brought down a peg. Turns out he wasn't invincible. He'd always loomed so large in Eli's life, his disappointment such a heavy weight, that it was surreal to see he was human after all.

"I see you smirking," Coach grumbled, but he didn't sound angry. "You like seeing me in pain?"

"Honestly, Bill. Of course he doesn't," his mom said, giving Coach a quick hug with one arm before handing him a glass of orange juice. "Now, drink up so you can take a pain pill. If you'd just called out, I would have brought it to your room."

"Tired of being cooped up in there. I'm going crazy." Coach took the juice and the pill his wife held out, keeping one hand on the walker as he tossed the pill in his mouth and gulped the OJ. "*Now* can I have some bacon? And coffee?"

Eli's mom nodded. "You should get that leg up, though."

"It's been a week. I don't have to keep it elevated all the time," he grumbled, but he turned and using the walker, shuffled back toward the living room.

Eli rinsed his plate and followed, watching as his father settled into his recliner, his mother adding a couple of pillows to prop his leg up higher.

"How long until you're in fighting form again?" Eli asked.

"Six weeks of physical therapy," his mom said.

"That's what they think," his dad countered. "I plan to do it in three."

His mother rolled her eyes before retreating to the kitchen and returning with a breakfast plate and mug of coffee. Coach shifted, getting comfortable, and sat the plate on his lap. Eli hesitated nearby, unsure of what to do. He and his father hadn't had a lot in common even before their falling out over his sexuality. Coach had wanted an athletic kid, someone he could put on sports teams. Eli had bowed out after his first bloody nose while playing peewee football. He'd stubbornly refused to play soccer, and he'd lasted only one season of tee-ball. Bad enough he wouldn't play sports, but he'd never cared to watch them either.

"Take a seat, Eli, unless you're planning on running off for another eight years."

"Bill, stop it," Eli's mother scolded. "Eli's here now, and if we want him to come back, we have to all work to understand each other better."

Eli sat on the sofa, too tense to relax into the cushions. His father's emotional greeting the night before had clearly been surprise. In the light of day, he was the same gruff asshole he'd always been.

"The way I remember it, I wasn't welcome here," Eli said quietly. "You gave me a choice, and I made it."

"To be with men," his father said.

"To be me."

"Eli, we love you," his mother said quickly. "Just as you are." A hint of steel entered her voice. "Right, Bill?"

His father nodded. "I always loved the boy. That was never in question."

"Could have fooled me," Eli muttered.

His father's eyes turned to him. "Well, I never meant for you to doubt it," he said. "You're my son, and you're always welcome home."

Eli nodded. "Okay. Thanks."

His mother smiled. "Well, now, that's better. I have to go clean up in the kitchen."

"I'll help," Eli said.

"No, no. Stay. Spend some time with your father," she said. "You must have a lot to catch up on."

She left the room, and Eli and his father exchanged an uncomfortable look.

"TV?" his dad asked.

"Yeah," Eli agreed quickly. "Netflix?"

"I usually watch the NFL Network."

Eli almost gave in, but the idea of watching sportscasters ramble on all morning did not appeal. "You ever watch the *Stargate* reruns?"

His father perked up. "I haven't thought about that show in years. Go on then, see if you can find it," he said, handing over the remote.

Eli finally relaxed enough to sink into the cushions as he punched remote buttons. He and his father wouldn't magically be on the same page overnight. But maybe they could find a way to co-exist peacefully.

4

"Eli, you should go change. Turner will be here soon."

Eli glanced down at his clothes — gray sweats and a white T-shirt — and self-consciously ran a hand through his hair to smooth it. When he realized what he was doing, he grimaced. He was not going to fall into the trap of longing for a straight guy, especially one who had already rejected him.

"I don't need to dress up for Turner," he said.

His mother chuckled. "Well, I know that. But you might want to wear something else to go to the Christmas tree farm. Turner agreed to get us a tree, and now that you're here, it'd be nice if you helped him. I told him to stop by right after school."

Eli glanced at the time on his cell phone. He had a few texts from Barb he needed to answer, as well as one from his roommate back in California. It was 3:30 p.m. now. It was nearly the end of the semester, so team practices would be over, but surely Turner had paperwork or something to do before he left?

"I can get the tree. Call and let Turner know I'm fine on my own," Eli said, retreating to his room. His mother called after him, but he ignored her in favor of changing.

Part of him wanted to see Turner again, but the other part
wanted to prove he was capable of taking care of his family as
much as Turner ever had. Eli knew it was irrational. He'd stayed
away intentionally, and he shouldn't feel guilty. Coach was ordinarily capable of getting his own Christmas tree, for one thing.
For another, his father had given him the ultimatum that drove
him away. But he couldn't shake the feeling he'd neglected his
parents for too long, that he should have tried sooner to mend
fences. They weren't getting any younger.

Eli dug through his bag to pull out a pair of faded jeans and a
long-sleeve T. He didn't have many winter-season clothes
anymore. No thermal shirts or sweaters; no heavy coats. A hoodie
would have to do. He pulled on a dark green one with the Los
Angeles National Forest logo on it. He had a white one with a big
rainbow and the logo for Rainbow Haven, but he wasn't looking
to get bashed.

Grabbing his keys and wallet, he headed to the living room.

"Eli," his mother said. "Why don't you wait for Turner? It'll be
easier with two pairs of hands."

"Turner would have been getting the tree on his own if I
wasn't here. And Coach has probably gotten it on his own plenty
of times."

"Yes, but—"

"Let the boy get a tree," Coach spoke up from his recliner,
startling Eli. His father had been dozing for the past hour, but
now he watched them from heavy eyes.

His mother threw up her hands. "Men. You always have something to prove, don't you?"

"I'm just getting a tree for my parents," Eli said. "It's no big
deal. Okay?"

She nodded. "You remember how to get to the Waits Winter
Tree Farm?" she asked. "We always get our tree there."

"I remember."

The Waits had struggled to keep their business afloat for a while, and Coach had launched a campaign to get the whole town out to support them. They'd since rebounded, but every year, the Harps returned to Waits Winter Farm for their tree. His father wouldn't have it any other way.

Eli kissed his mother's cheek, nodded to his father, and headed out the door. As he opened the garage and got into his cold car, he thought this might have been the first time in his life that his father took his side in something.

Even something as silly as arguing over a Christmas tree.

Turner had just started up his Jeep Wrangler, cranking the heater on high and setting it to defrost, when he got a call from Molly. "Hey, I'm just leaving," he said.

"Eli went to get the tree on his own," she said. "I'm sorry for changing plans on you at the last minute."

"That's okay," he said. Then hesitated. "He's going out to the Waits tree farm?"

"Yes."

"What did he drive? Coach's truck?"

There was a small exhale on the line. "Oh, no. No, he took his car. It's a cute little convertible. It's not going to be able to get down that country road with all this snow, is it? It probably hasn't been cleared. I should have thought of that."

"Some of it may have melted off," Turner said, though he didn't really believe that.

Most of the city streets were clear, but they'd been cleared by snowplows and driven over a few hundred times since the snowfall. Country roads were some of the last to be cleared, if they were at all, with weather like this. And with less traffic, the snow wouldn't melt off as fast.

"Turner, could you—"

"I'll drive out that way," he said at the same time.

"Thank you," Molly said. "You're the sweetest. I don't know why Eli had to be so stubborn. And his father was no help. *Let the boy go get a tree,* he said. Sometimes men are ridiculous. Oh, present company excluded of course."

"Of course." Turner smiled at the exasperation in her voice. He wasn't all that surprised Coach had endorsed Eli's macho pride. He was probably over the moon to see it. "I was planning to go anyway, so it's no trouble."

"You're wonderful. I'll thank you with dinner. I've made a huge pot of chili. Oh! Your family too. I'll call Daisy right now. We can make a night of decorating the tree. It'll be fun."

Turner shifted his truck into drive. "That's a great idea, Molly. Mom will love that."

Hopefully seeing Molly in her usual cheerful form would reassure his mother that she didn't need to fret about Christmas Day, too.

After saying good-bye, Turner turned his Jeep in the direction of the tree farm east of town. With any luck, Eli would be fine and Turner would drive right on by so he could assert his independence or whatever the hell he was doing. If Eli was anything like Turner remembered, he wouldn't be too pleased to have Turner checking up on him, but better safe than sorry.

———

Eli thumped his head onto the steering wheel. "Shit!"

Outside his window, the world was sparkling, the late afternoon sunlight bouncing off a blanket of snow covering the ground and frosting evergreen trees. He'd made it most of the way to the tree farm without incident — until this godforsaken road between towering pines.

Juniper was actually named for the smaller western juniper trees found in the high desert region of the state, but the Waits farm was east of town — closer to the Ochoco National Forest — where ponderosa pines emerged to stand sentinel over the landscape. Eli had turned off the highway onto a rural road. Well, really, road was a generous term. Right now, packed with snow as it was, it looked more like a trail meandering through the forest. A set of tire tracks ran down the center of the road, the ruts providing a path through the snow. Eli had followed them, avoiding the deeper now, but then he hit a damn dip, the car bounced out of the ruts, and he'd swerved into a deep drift of snow on the edge of the road.

Juniper hadn't gotten that much snowfall. Not enough for three-foot snowdrifts, but the wind must have blown snow around so that it built up along the edge of the road. And now Eli was screwed.

He'd spun his wheels for a good five minutes trying to get free. He'd shifted into drive, then reverse, then drive, trying to rock his way out. He didn't have a shovel to dig out the tires, so he'd found an old drive-through cup and tried to use it to scoop away the snow until his hands burned like fire from the cold.

Now, he sat shivering and defeated, red hands pressed to the heater vents. His feet and legs were faring only a little better, with snow caked to his shoes, soaking his socks, and clinging to his jeans.

Life fail, he thought. *What's fucking new?*

He'd have to call for a tow. He fumbled for his phone when a tapping on the driver's-side window made him jump. He hit the button to lower it with numb fingers to see Turner looking down at him.

"You're a menace," he said.

Eli looked miserable. His nose was beet red, giving Rudolph a good run for lead reindeer. His cheeks were rosy too. His hair was messy and windblown, and not in a stylish way, and his hands looked raw and chapped from the cold.

"Jesus Christ, Eli," Turner groused. "My driver's ed students would know better than to take a little car like this down a snow-packed country road. Where did you learn to drive?"

"Not from you, obviously," Eli muttered.

It had been a rhetorical question. They'd learned to drive together, though Eli had obviously forgotten a few key lessons.

Turner opened Eli's door. "Come on. Let's get you in my Jeep and get you warmed up. Then we can talk about how you almost ran one of my students off the road yesterday."

Eli turned the key in the ignition with shaking hands. "I... what?"

He looked honestly surprised. At least it hadn't been an intentionally dick move then.

"Jeep," Turner said. "You look like you're freezing. Doesn't your heater work?"

Eli climbed out, shoulders hunching against the cold, and Turner put an arm around his shoulders, turning him toward the truck. He did it instinctively, wanting to shelter Eli from the cold, and he wasn't prepared for how he felt as Eli huddled against his side as they walked.

He fit under Turner's arm perfectly, and the weight of him — even through the bulk of Turner's coat — was enough to make his heart flutter.

He opened the door for Eli, then resisted the urge to help him into the Jeep. He wasn't helpless, just cold and miserable. Turner circled the Jeep and got in on his own side. It was toasty warm inside because he'd left the engine running, and Turner pulled off his own gloves to take Eli's reddened hands in his and rub some warmth into them. "Jesus, your hands are like ice."

"Didn't have a shovel," Eli said. "I was trying to dig out."

Turner skimmed his gaze over Eli, from his inadequate hoodie to his damp jeans and soaking feet.

Apparently in Eli's case, you can take the boy out of Oregon *and* take Oregon out of the boy. Because he looked like a Californian who didn't know how to drive or dress for the weather.

"Did you forget we wear coats and gloves around here?" he asked, lifting Eli's right hand to blow hot breath over his palm.

Eli swallowed and looked away. "I didn't have any with me," he said. "And I wasn't planning on getting stuck in the snow."

"You should have been with that car."

Eli turned to him, eyes narrowed. "Are you done giving me shit? I need to call a tow truck."

Turner took in the angry expression, easily seeing through it. Eli was embarrassed. Based on what Molly said, he'd been trying to prove something by going on his own. Either to himself or to Coach. Or even to Turner.

"Yeah, I'm done. But you don't need to call for a tow. I can pull you out with the Jeep. It's got a winch on the front."

Eli pulled his hands from Turner's and ran them through his hair. "That sounds ... like the best idea I've ever heard."

Turner chuckled. "You're really gonna love my next one then."

"What's that?"

"I've got some dry socks for you."

"My hero," Eli said playfully, making more flutters erupt inside Turner. If he wasn't careful, he was going to be harvesting butterflies.

Turner turned in his seat, straining to grab the gym bag from the back seat. He preferred to run, but he still hit the weights a couple of times a week to keep up his muscle tone. And to work off sexual frustration. Occasionally, he and Desiree — the physical education teacher — fell into bed together, but they'd both agreed they weren't compatible enough for a serious relationship. He'd been trying to break the habit of having sex with her because while it was nice to have the release, he inevitably felt lonelier afterward, more aware of the one thing his life was missing.

He'd tried dating. He'd mostly hooked up in college, but he'd had two relationships in Juniper since he'd returned. Neither had gone well, in the sense they'd broken up, but he'd managed to stay on friendly terms with them both. Too friendly in Desiree's case, maybe.

Turner unzipped the bag and tossed a pair of socks into Eli's lap.

"How clean are these?" Eli asked.

"They're dry," Turner said.

"Right," Eli said, leaning down to tug off his shoes and socks. "Beggars and choosers, I guess."

Turner grinned. "Wearing my sweat won't kill you."

Eli glanced up at him through dark, thick eyelashes. He didn't say anything, but the curve of his lips gave away that his mind had gone to exactly the place Turner's had at that comment. Jesus, what was wrong with him, flirting with Eli like that? They hadn't even fixed their friendship, and he was already thinking with his dick.

Eli pulled on the white, cotton socks, then held his shoes up to the heating vent. They wouldn't have time to dry, but maybe they'd warm a bit. "What now?"

Turner leaned forward, nudging Eli back to pop open the glovebox. He had a spare pair of gloves and a beanie. He passed Eli the gloves, then tugged the hat over Eli's hair himself, taking a few moments to adjust it to give him an excuse to touch Eli. "There. I don't have a coat to spare, unfortunately."

Eli's bright green eyes met his. "Thanks for all this."

Turner only smiled. "What are friends for?"

He dropped his hands reluctantly as Eli looked at him solemnly. "Are we still friends?"

Turner's heart squeezed hard in his chest. "I'd like to be."

Eli broke eye contact, turning to look out the window. He nodded once. "Me too."

"Then we are," Turner said, squeezing Eli's shoulder once, before pulling out into the road again.

"What about my car?"

"We'll get it on the way home. We should get to the farm. Your mom is inviting my family over for a dinner-and-decorating party, and something tells me it won't work too well without a Christmas tree."

Eli chuckled, but there was a bitter quality to it. "Leave it to me to fuck everything up. Just like old times."

"Bullshit," Turner said. When Eli looked startled, he added more gently, "You never fucked anything up back then."

"I did, according to Coach."

"Coach is an asshole."

Eli gave him a challenging look. "And yet you work for him. Help him out in tough times. You're *family*, you said."

"We are family," Turner said. "But we don't always like our family. And believe me, Coach knows how I feel about the way he treated you."

"He does?" Eli said, clearly surprised.

Turner nodded. "I texted you once while you were in college, do you remember? I wanted to know if you were coming home for Christmas."

Eli nodded. He and Turner had tried to maintain their friendship for a while, but it had never been the same after the Christmas kiss fiasco.

"I remember. I told you I wasn't going home because my father told me I was only welcome there if I wasn't gay."

Turner nodded. "I got so pissed, I went over to your house and told Coach he was a bastard."

Eli's eyes widened. "You didn't."

Turner chuckled. "I did. We had a good, old-fashioned yelling match. Your mom was crying." He grimaced. "Sorry about that."

"So, what happened?"

"Well, he told me to mind my own business, and I told him you would always be my business."

Turner's throat grew tight just remembering that night. Finding out he wouldn't get the chance to see Eli, much less fix their friendship, had been heartbreaking.

Are you a fag too? Coach had asked him. *You're awfully upset my boy's gone.*

What if I were? Turner had shouted. *Does that change the fact I was your star runner? That I went to college on a track scholarship? Would it change who I am?*

It changes a lot of things, Turner. It changes how everyone else in the world sees you.

Maybe the world shouldn't care so much who I date. Or who Eli dates. Maybe it's not the world's fucking business.

Coach had nodded. *Maybe not, but Eli made it everyone's business when he came out. You can't have it both ways.*

Eli didn't want to lie about who he was. That's not the same as someone judging him for being gay. You know what, never mind. You don't get it. Regardless of what the world thinks, you're his father. You could have stuck by him. Now, he's not coming home because of you. What if he never comes back?

He'll come back, Coach said dismissively.

What if he doesn't?

He will, Coach said a little uncertainly as Molly cried silently in the background. She'd fought for Eli too, Turner knew, and Coach wouldn't keep Eli from coming home. But the damage had been done. Because Eli didn't come home that year, or any other year — until now.

"Wow," Eli said, bringing him back to the present. "I, uh, didn't know you cared that much. I mean, our friendship was ..."

"I know," Turner managed. "But a lifetime of friendship shouldn't fall apart because of one wrong turn, right?"

"I guess not," Eli murmured. "We were just so dumb."

"Incredibly dumb," Turner agreed, his heart feeling lighter.

Maybe he and Eli could find their way back to being friends. It would take time to get back to where they once were, if it was possible at all. But any form of friendship would be better than what they'd had for the past eight years.

5

Eli still felt like an idiot as Turner pulled in at the tree farm, but at least he was a warm idiot. He'd kept his hands and sleeves in front of the heating vents, and his skin was back to a normal shade of peach. His sleeves were dry now, and even if he couldn't say the same for his shoes, at least he had dry socks. Turner's old gym socks, which absolutely should not be a turn-on. It should be gross. But the way Turner had cracked that joke about wearing his sweat...

Well, Eli was a healthy gay man. He might not want to get hung up on Turner again, but that didn't mean the man wasn't ten kinds of gorgeous. He looked different than he had in high school. He wore a short beard, just enough to surpass scruffy, and he'd lost the lankiness of youth in exchange for the brawniness of a man who was in his prime. His hair, too, had darkened a shade from sandy blond to brown. It was in his eyes that Eli saw the Turner he'd always known. And in his expressions; he had the same quirk to his lips when he was amused, and the same wrinkle in his forehead when he was worried.

Only a small, flimsy sign marked the turn into the Waits farm, but Eli could see the large farmhouse in the distance, framed by two massive pines that had been decorated with lights he could barely make out in the daylight but which must be gorgeous at night. Each tree was topped with a gold star.

Large wreaths decorated the massive front porch, hanging from the railing that ran along its length. Eli remembered that they were for sale, and that if you went into the house, its living room was actually a holiday craft store filled with Christmas tree ornaments and other decorations. They were particularly known for their angels. Angels made from wood, angels made from tin, angel wind chimes, and angel tree toppers. There were Santas, snowmen, and reindeer in the mix too, but their selection of angels was remarkable, if you liked that kind of thing. And Eli's mother did.

Just behind the house, the tree farm started. Neat rows of trees — divided into three sections: Douglas Fir, Noble Fir, and Fraser — stretched as far as the eye could see.

Turner parked on a patch of open field, and Eli tugged on the spare gloves Turner had given him. They were a little big, but they'd do. Then he tugged up his hood over his beanie and stepped out on ground that had been mostly cleared of snow.

"They cleared the parking lot, but not the road leading up to it?"

Turner smirked. "If you get stuck on their land, it's their problem. Besides, they're not responsible for a county road."

Eli and Turner crossed the large lot — really just an open patch of land — and made their way around the farmhouse to the trees. There were a handful of cars, but the tree farm probably saw more business on the weekends. During its busiest times, the farm was filled with families not only shopping for a tree, but also purchasing holiday crafts and hot cider from the store. The Waits kept a horse-drawn wagon, which would cart people around the farm so they could look at the trees further afield and enjoy the scenery.

But today, Eli and Turner didn't have the time or inclination to indulge in holiday fun. They were there to get their tree and get home, where Eli would no doubt face the disappointment of his father for failing to be a real man once again. If he was lucky, it would be a silent censure rather than the biting remarks his father made when he was a teen. Coach had made an effort to get along with Eli since he'd arrived, but he kept waiting for the other shoe to drop.

"My parents still like the Douglas fir?" he asked.

Turner nodded. "Yep."

Eli blew out a breath, oddly reassured that his parents hadn't changed their tree preference. It made him feel like maybe he still knew them. His mom still baked; his father still watched football; and they still liked Douglas firs from Waits Winter Tree Farm. He'd stayed away for years, and he felt millions of years removed from the person he'd been when he lived in Juniper, but his parents were the same people despite a few new gray hairs.

A dark-haired man whose beard put Turner's to shame came around the corner. He wore a heavy flannel jacket, jeans, and work boots. He paused, eyes roaming over them, and broke into a grin. "Well, if it isn't Turner and ..." He paused. "Oh, hell, is that Eli Harp?"

Eli smiled quizzically. "Um, yes? Hi."

"Damn boy. You done grown up!"

Eli blinked, at a loss, until Turner heaved a sigh and said, "Eli, this is Cam Waits. You remember him from school?"

Eli gaped, astounded. Cam Waits had been a heartthrob in high school, one of those guys who was always starring in the school plays. He'd had a baby face and a much narrower frame. Now, with his broad shoulders and thick beard, he was the picture of the stereotypical lumberjack.

"No, really?"

Cam chuckled. "Yeah, I was a late bloomer. Grew some hair on my chest. And my face. Now I'm a regular mountain man," he said with a wink. "All I need is some moonshine to complete the picture."

"Cam thinks he's funny," Turner said. Then he turned to Cam: "Eli's folks need a Douglas fir."

"I think we've got one or two left," Cam said, gesturing toward the rows of trees. "You know the drill. We can cut the tree for you, or—"

"Just get us a handsaw. I've got twine to tie it down."

Cam led them to a small toolshed a few feet from where the trees grew. He went inside, returning with a simple handsaw that he handed to Turner. Then, turning to Eli, he said, "It's sure good seeing you back here, Eli. I know your last couple of years were rough, but I always admired your bravery."

"Uh, thanks," Eli said, thrown by the compliment. He'd never seen his coming out as anything other than a bad decision in retrospect. "I wasn't brave, though. Just naïve."

"Well, still, you set an example for those who came after you. Juniper is a better place because of it."

Eli was skeptical. "I've been gone a long time. If Juniper has changed, it doesn't have anything to do with me. I just want to live my life."

Cam grinned at him. "Don't we all?"

Turner hefted the saw in his hand. "We better get that tree."

"Sure, sure," Cam said easily. But as Turner charged into the grove of evergreens, Cam fell into step beside Eli.

"Where have you been then?" he asked.

"California."

Cam's eyes brightened. "San Fran?"

Eli shook his head. "No, I wish. I live in Northern California, in an area not a lot more liberal than Juniper."

"Why there then?"

Turner continued to walk ahead, but Eli sensed he was listening to them. "Because it wasn't here? I don't know. I went into marketing in college, and I got an internship in a small town in California. I liked it, and they liked me, so when I graduated, they offered me a permanent position."

"So, you do marketing for a big business or something?"

Based on Cam's comments about Eli's last years, he figured he was safe to talk about his job. "A youth shelter, actually. For LGBTQ kids."

"A shelter? You mean ..."

"Yeah, even in California, some parents don't accept their children." His chest tightened as it always did. This topic was so close to home. Coach hadn't thrown him out, but he'd emotionally disowned him long before he gave him an ultimatum not to come back until he changed his ways. It was part of the reason he'd been drawn to working at Rainbow Haven — and just about the only reason he'd settled in another conservative place rather than seeking out a more liberal community.

"That's a goddamn shame," Cam said.

Turner had stopped and turned, his eyes on Eli. "Molly never mentioned your job, other than to say you were in marketing. That's really something."

Eli shrugged. "Guess we didn't talk about my job much. Mostly she wanted to know about my personal life. Did I have a boyfriend? Was I happy? Would I please think about coming home and giving my dad a chance to apologize?"

"Did he apologize?" Turner asked.

"Not in so many words," Eli said. "But probably the closest to an apology he's ever come."

"That's something."

"Yeah."

"Well, I think what you do is amazing," Cam said brightly, lifting the somber mood. "I'd love to hear more about it. Maybe we could get a drink and catch up?"

"Oh. Um—"

"We've got to get this tree back and decorated. Eli's mother is making dinner, so..."

"Well, not right now," Cam said with a grin. "How about Saturday night? I'll need a beer or ten after dealing with the weekend crowd."

Eli and Cam had never been friends in high school, but he'd never had a problem with him either. Not like with some. And there was an interested gleam in his eye that had Eli wondering ... was Cam Waits gay?

"I could grab a beer. Sure."

"Me too," Turner said, surprising him. "Eli and I can meet you at the pub."

Cam's gaze flicked between them, and he smiled. "Back to being hitched at the hip, eh? Sounds good. I'll buy the first round."

Okay, maybe he's not gay. Cam waved goodbye, still smiling, and sauntered off. He didn't seem to mind that Turner was going, and when Eli ran his words back through his head, he realized that Cam hadn't specifically asked Eli out.

Clearly, you've gone too long without sex and are now imagining sexy lumberjacks want you.

Eli watched Cam trudge back the way they'd come until Turner cleared his throat. "Tree?"

"Right," Eli said, turning back to the task at hand. Looking around, he saw that every tree looked full-limbed and richly green. "They all look great. Let's just pick one."

"It's your house."

Eli wandered a few feet and stopped in front of full-bodied Douglas fir, pointing.

"Good choice," Turner said, and bent down to saw through the thin trunk. Eli kept a hand on the tree, gloves protecting his hands from prickly pine needles, as Turner worked.

"Do you not like Cam?" he asked, wondering at Turner's weird mood during that last conversation.

Turner's sawing paused for a fraction of a second before he resumed. "I like Cam fine."

"You seemed a little ... annoyed?"

Turner gave one last forceful pull of the saw and the tree gave, falling to the side. Eli caught the top and Turner grabbed hold of the bottom, lifting it so they could carry the tree out together.

Turner met his eyes over the tree. "I like Cam. I like you. I like everybody, all right?"

Eli's lips twitched. "All right. Your heart is huge. I get it."

Turner smiled slowly, making Eli's heart skip a beat. "I've never had any complaints. About any of my huge ... parts."

Eli rolled his eyes. "Don't brag about it unless you plan to use it."

"What, my heart?" Turner asked, sounding startled.

"Your anything." Eli said, feeling his face heat despite the cool weather. He'd meant to make a joke, not imply Turner should be using his heart with him. Or his dick. Or anything at all, for that matter. "Weren't we talking about Cam?"

Turner snorted. "I don't have a problem with Cam," he said, but his glower wasn't the most convincing. There was something about Cam that bothered him, even if he wouldn't say what it was. Eli decided to quit while he was ahead and focused on carrying the tree.

Molly held the door open as they carried the tree inside. Turner had stopped and used his winch to pull Eli's Camaro out of the snowbank, and he'd followed him back to his parents' house. Despite returning with his car none the worse for wear, his parents would undoubtedly ask why Turner was there when Eli had said he'd handle the tree.

"Aw, it's beautiful," Molly said. "You boys picked a good one. Isn't it a lovely tree, Bill?"

Eli's father grunted from his corner of the room. He usually loved going all out for Christmas, but his interests had always laid with the exterior decorations: the large, greeting card display they usually had out front along with lights on the house. None of which had been done this year. Maybe Eli could get to that before Christmas Day. He'd hated setting up that plywood card, but it had to be bugging his dad that it wasn't out there. He'd always been one of the first to put his out.

"I've cleared out the corner by the fireplace," Molly said, pointing to the space opposite Coach's recliner. Considering there'd been a table there earlier in the day, the empty floor space was noticeable enough they'd already begun to carry the tree that way. A tree stand stood in the center of the space with a tree blanket wrapped around it.

While they struggled to get the tree screwed in, Eli crouching under the tree while Turner held it straight, his father brought up the inevitable. "I thought you went out to the farm alone, Eli."

"Yeah, I did, but..."

"I ran into him outside," Turner said. "Figured since I was here, I might as well help set up the tree."

"So, your car made it?" Molly asked. "I should have stopped you." She tsked. "You didn't even have on a proper jacket. Shows what kind of Mom I am."

Eli finished tightening the last bolt and scooted out from under the tree. He wrapped an arm around his mother, drawing her in against him much as Turner had done for him outside his car on the side of the road. "I'm a grown-up. It's hardly your job to make sure I wear my mittens."

She sniffed. "You'll always be my baby, Eli." She pulled back to look up at him. "Even when you stay away, you're my son."

Eli sighed, but he couldn't help smiling. "I know, Mom. But you have plenty on your mind. I can take care of myself."

He glanced at Turner, wondering if he was biting his tongue not to mention that Eli hadn't done such a great job of that today.

"Listen to Eli," Coach said gruffly. "You've always coddled him. That's half the problem—"

He stopped abruptly. "Half the problem?" Eli said, even though he knew he shouldn't. "Is there a problem with me?"

"I didn't mean it like that."

"Because if you think me being gay is a problem, you sure as hell shouldn't be blaming Mom for that."

"Eli," she said, tugging on his arm. "Don't."

"No," Eli said, too angry to pacify his father. "I think we should clear the air. I'm gay. I was born that way. If you think Mom was too soft on me, you made up for it. All the football you made me play and then watch, the admonishments to just toughen up, the insults that I was an embarrassment to men everywhere. None of that made me straight, so why do you think a mother's love would make me gay?"

"I didn't mean it that way," Coach practically growled. His face was red, his eyes glittering. "You could be stronger, more independent. That's what I meant. It's not about being gay."

"Isn't it?" Eli challenged. "I've lived on my own since I graduated high school. What about that isn't independent?"

His father didn't answer.

"Well?" Eli pressed.

Turner, who had up until now remained quiet, cleared his throat. "I thought I'd go get Scout, if it's all right for him to come over? I don't like to leave him cooped up too long."

"Oh, of course," Molly said quickly, seizing on a change in topic.

"Scout's always welcome here," Coach said.

"Unlike your son," Eli muttered under his breath.

"Eli," Turner said firmly, "why don't you come with me? I can show you my place."

Eli lifted an eyebrow.

"And lend you a coat to use while you're here," Turner added, as if he thought Eli might get the wrong idea from the invitation. *If only.*

"Okay," Eli said. "If you don't need me for anything, Mom?"

"Go with Turner," Molly said. "I've got the chili bubbling away. There's nothing much to do but decorate the tree, and I'm saving that for after dinner."

Eli nodded. "Okay then."

"Eli," his father said before he turned to the door.

"Yeah?"

"The tree looks good, nice full branches. You even got it standing straight. That's quite the feat." He attempted a smile.

Eli felt the knot in his chest loosen. His dad wasn't there yet, but he was trying.

6

Scout barked sharply behind the front door of Turner's bungalow. The house had once been painted a cheery yellow, but it had faded to a cream color and was cracked and peeling. Turner had never been as aware of its fading glory as he was today, with Eli looked upon it for the first time. Turner figured the houses in California had a bit more curb appeal.

"Scout, hush," he called through the door as he put his key into the lock. "It's me."

The barks gave way to eager whines and whimpers. Poor dog had been cooped up too much lately now that team practices were over for the season. He was used to running with the kids every afternoon.

Scout jumped forward eagerly as the door opened, giving another sharp bark. He wasn't barking at Eli so much as expressing excitement, which he emphasized with his wagging tail.

"Well, hello again," Eli said as Scout nosed at his hand and then gave it a lick while Turner rubbed his ears.

"You two-timer," Turner scolded in a light tone. "I bring a guy home and you love him more than me?"

As if Scout understood, he whirled and jumped up on his hind feet. Turner caught his paws. "Uh-uh. Down. Let's get you some grub."

Turner went to the kitchen, where he scooped some dog food into a dish. Scout beat him there, watching his every move with a hungry gleam in his eye. As soon as the food was in the dish, he fell on it with gusto, crunching happily.

Eli lingered in the doorway, looking around. Turner became hyperaware of the flaws in his house he tended to overlook most of the time: the peeling wallpaper, the scuffed floors, the water stain on the ceiling. At least he was relatively tidy, with only a bit of clutter on the kitchen counters, and that was mainly because the place was so small he had no storage.

Turner cleared his throat. "It's a rental."

"Oh, yeah? Better than an apartment."

"Definitely better for Scout," Turner agreed, "but it could use some TLC."

Eli half turned to look back into the living room, where a black leather sofa and armchair were positioned in front of a flat-screen television hanging on the wall. A large poinsettia sat on the table next to the sofa, an attempt to dress up the room for the holidays, with the two presents Turner had managed to wrap so far, along with a large box of assorted chocolates he'd bought for his sister. There wasn't much else to see. He hadn't bothered with a tree since he'd be spending Christmas Day with the Harps.

"It's nice," Eli said, his gaze flicking from the furnishings to the wooden floors to the large, wood-framed window looking out on the front yard. "At least it has some character, unlike the apartment where I live."

Turner smiled ruefully. "Your apartment was probably built after the 1920s," he said. "This place is pretty small. But it's just me, so ..."

Eli glanced back to him. "My building is newer, but also so

white." He gave a shudder. "Cream carpeting, white walls. No woodwork to be seen. Besides, I'd love to live alone."

That got Turner's attention. "You don't live alone?"

Eli shook his head. "I live with Levi. He's not the tidiest guy, either. There's a lot to be said for having your own domain, huh?"

"Yeah." Turner fought the urge to ask Eli about Levi. He was ninety percent sure Levi was just a roommate. Eli didn't sound particularly fond of living with him. Okay, eighty percent sure, because what couple didn't make jokes about the pet peeves of cohabitating?

It doesn't matter, Turner reminded himself. *Eli's home for vacation, and then he'll leave again. His love life is his business.*

Turner cleared his throat. "I need a shower. You okay to wait?"

"Sure," Eli said with a grin. "I'll just get to know Scout a little better."

Turner approached the kitchen doorway, turning to squeeze past Eli, their clothes brushing as he went. Eli's eyes met his, just for a moment as he passed, and Turner felt the flare of attraction between them. It hadn't dulled with time or distance. If anything, Turner was even more drawn to Eli now that he had fully accepted his own sexuality. Without fear and anxiety clouding his senses, the desire that thrummed through him was more difficult to ignore.

He headed for the bathroom before he did something foolish. "Feel free to grab a drink or watch TV," he said. "Whatever you want."

"Okay, I'll snoop through all your stuff," Eli joked.

Turner laughed. "Oh no, you might find my collection of porn."

"Don't you keep it on your computer like a normal man? Besides, I doubt we have the same taste in porn."

Depends on the day, Turner thought. He had a feeling he'd be in the mood for gay porn this holiday season.

Eli didn't snoop ... much. For one thing, there wasn't much to snoop through. Not unless he went into Turner's bedroom, and that seemed like a terrible idea. He did take a peek at his junk mail. Judging by the advertisements, Turner wore Calvin Klein underwear. He also got a lot of ads for activewear, but that was no surprise. That he had a mailer from an LGBT organization, thanking him for his donation, was more surprising, though Eli knew Turner had always been open-minded.

He opened a few kitchen cabinets, noting that Turner still had a sweet spot for Pop-Tarts despite being cut enough that Eli was pretty sure anything he threw at Turner would just bounce right off that tight muscle. He'd love to bounce on that muscle ...

Not going there.

Scout nudged his knee, and Eli looked down to see him panting happily, the black-and-white fur around his mouth still wet from the water bowl.

"Hey, buddy."

Eli started to pet him, which evolved into some playful ear-tugging, and he moved out of the kitchen so they'd have more space to rough-house. Eli bent over behind the sofa, patting Scout's side and encouraging him to pounce around playfully. They were midwrestle when Turner stepped out of the bathroom, wrapped in a towel.

Holy. Hell.

Eli had not been imagining the muscle under those clothes. The man was fine. Eli had thought he was hot in high school, but this was a whole other level of delicious man. And he did mean *man*. The thick pelt of hair on Turner's chest that narrowed to a thin line down his navel hadn't been there the last time Eli saw him shirtless. His chest was broader, his pecs more defined and tipped with nipples growing hard in the cool air of the hallway.

Eli sat back on his heels, dumbfounded, and just drank him in while Scout nosed at Eli's hand, trying to regain his attention. *Sorry, dog, not happening.*

Turner shivered, then crossed his arms over his chest. "I'll just be a minute."

His eyes shot up to Turner's. *Busted.*

Eli shrugged and bit his bottom lip, unable to keep his eyes from one more slide over Turner's body. He'd been hung up on Turner's chest before, but now his gaze dropped to muscled thighs and calves. Those powerful runner's legs. He undoubtedly had a great ass too. Damn.

"Take your time," Eli said. "I've got nowhere to be."

Turner blushed and went through a door to his right. Why had he stayed there, with Eli staring, when his room was so close? Maybe he'd simply been caught off-guard by Eli's perusal. But it wasn't as if Turner didn't know how Eli felt back in the day. That stupid kiss under the mistletoe was the most obvious clue that Eli wanted him, but it wasn't the only one. He'd been a drooling puppy, and Turner had been the boy he adored.

Eli shook off the ludicrous thought that Turner had paused there purposely to let Eli look his fill, turning his attention back to Scout. *You will not entertain fantasies about a straight man. Not ever again.*

Turner tugged on jeans and a sweater, fighting the blood rushing south to his cock. "Not now," he muttered. "You are headed to a holiday dinner for fuck's sake."

His dick didn't care. It thickened at the memory of Eli staring at him boldly and biting down on his lip like a goddamn wet dream. With a curse under his breath, Turner crammed himself into his pants and finished dressing.

His phone rang, sufficiently distracting him from more lusty thoughts. "Hey, sis."

"Hey, Turner. I'm picking up Cassie from play auditions and heading over to the Harps, but can you get Mom? It's out of the way, and we have a full car."

"Oh, sure. Play the single-mom-with-a-car-full-of-kids card. I see how it is."

Krystal laughed. "Well, you could buy me a larger vehicle."

"Don't think I haven't considered it," he joked.

Picking up his mom wasn't ideal. He'd hoped to steal a few more minutes alone with Eli, though God knew why. It wasn't as if he intended to start anything with him when he was only home for a short time. Turner was no stranger to casual sex, but sex with Eli would be anything but casual.

Turner agreed to pick up his mother, hung up the phone, and reached into his closet for a fleece pullover that had shrunk in the wash that he never wore anymore. Then he headed out to the living room.

Eli was on the sofa, tapping away on his phone. Probably with a *friend*.

Turner and Eli had managed an awkward friendship via texting and Facebook for a while after they left for college, but at some point Eli had unfriended Turner. That still stung.

"Here," he said, tossing his fleece down next to Eli. "It's warmer than a hoodie. No hood, but you can keep the beanie and gloves I gave you."

Eli glanced up with a distracted smile on his lips. *Who was he texting? Was it a guy?*

"Thanks." He tapped out one more line, tucked his phone in his back pocket, and pulled the fleece pullover on. When he stood, it hung a little low, down to his thigh. He didn't fill out the shoulders, being so slender, but it fit better than Turner had expected.

Something inside him glowed warm to see Eli in his jacket. He ignored the strange feeling and nodded toward the door. "You ready?"

"Yep."

"Come on, Scout. Let's go to Coach's house!" he said to his dog, who was leaning against Eli's thigh like a little traitor. Not that Turner could really blame him. Eli had a happy glow to him, some sort of magical beauty that came from within. Turner had always seen it, and as much as he'd tried, he'd never been totally immune.

Eli laughed as Scout barked once in excitement and ran to the door. "You take him over there a lot, huh?"

"Enough. More lately, since your dad's knee went wonky. He spent at least eight weeks limping around before he got surgery."

Eli winced. "Ouch. Well, thanks for looking after him."

Turner paused at the door. "He's not your responsibility. I know I was a little pissy about you being gone so long, but Coach has no one to blame for that but himself."

Eli's eyes met his. "Thank you for saying that."

Turner nodded, hesitated, then said, "But I want you to add me back on Facebook. I never stopped being your friend, and that *does* piss me off."

Eli's lips quirked with amusement. "Fair enough. I'll do it tonight."

Turner stared hard at him, but he seemed to mean it. Nodding once, Turner led the way out to the Jeep. "We have to make a quick stop to pick up my mother. Then, we can head back."

"Sounds good," Eli said. "I'll sit in back with Scout."

He probably preferred Scout, Turner thought with annoyance. Only to realize he was jealous of his own dog.

7

Turner stepped into the Harps' house, mouth watering at the smell of chili spices permeating the air. Christmas music tinkled through the living room from a Bluetooth speaker, and while the tree wasn't yet decorated, a short string of lights twinkled over the fireplace where the stockings were hung.

Scout bounded ahead, straight for the kitchen, his favorite place to be in this house. He knew where his bread was buttered, and Eli made a beeline for the coat closet, tugging the fleece jacket over his head and rucking up the back of his shirt in the process. He flashed a strip of pale skin, drawing Turner's gaze like a magnet.

"It smells good," Eli said.

"Better than good," Turner agreed.

Turner's mother, who'd hesitated near the front door, gave a little wave as Molly entered from the direction of the kitchen.

"Daisy, so good to see you," she said warmly, embracing Turner's mother, who was too thin for his liking. She fretted so much she often lost her appetite. She'd been prescribed some anti-anxiety medication after losing her husband, but her doctor had gradually weaned her off it. It might be time to discuss a return to medication. She worried more than was healthy.

Turner made a mental note to talk to Krystal about it later, turning to compliment Molly. "Thanks again for inviting us over. You make the best chili."

Molly smiled. "You're such a dear. You know you're welcome anytime, Turner." She looked at Turner's mother. "You too. You don't need an engraved invitation to stop by."

"Well, I know Coach is recovering." She glanced around. "Is he resting? Are we being too loud?"

Molly patted her arm. "You're fine. He's just dressing for dinner."

She guided Turner's mom into the dining room, talking about the holiday decorations for the tree she wanted to bring out later, and Turner exchanged a look with Eli.

"I'm sorry again about your father," Eli said. "What happened?"

"Aneurysm. While I was at Oregon State. He went quickly."

"I'm so sorry. I wish I could have been there for you."

Turner looked away, swallowing hard. "I was in my senior year of college, so when I graduated, I came home."

"That's why you're still in Juniper?"

Turner met his eye. "My family needs me, but I didn't hate Juniper like you did. I'm mostly happy here."

"Mostly?"

He shrugged. "Who's 100 percent happy anywhere? I like being close to my family. Juniper isn't a bad place."

"I never said it was."

Turner fixed him with a look. "But it's what you've always thought."

"Do you blame me?"

"No, I really don't, but you're not in high school anymore. There are good people here."

"And yet you went right back to that hell hole for a job."

Turner's jaw tightened. "I like my job, and I like the kids. I didn't plan to come back to Juniper, and I definitely didn't plan to spend my days at Juniper High, but I'm glad I ended up there because I can make sure it's a good place — a *safe* place — for all kids."

Just then Coach entered, breaking the gathering tension. Eli turned to his father. "Ready for some chili?"

His dad, dressed in dress slacks and a button-down that strained over his stomach, shuffled forward with his walker. "Born ready to eat your mother's cooking." He patted his stomach. "I used to look like Turner. Now, look at me."

Turner chuckled. "Oh, I'm sure you looked better than me."

Eli had his doubts, but he kept them to himself. There was no need to inform everyone in the room that Turner was the hottest man he'd ever seen.

The doorbell rang. "That'll be Krystal and the kids. Late as usual."

Eli opened the door, catching a glimpse of chestnut hair and a wide smile before he was yanked into a hug. "Eli, you rotten, no good, terrible man!" Krystal cried, shaking him a little as she pulled back. "You've been gone too long."

Eli grinned. "Sorry. But you were taken, so I had to run away and nurse my broken heart."

"I got married when you were ten."

"And I never recovered."

Krystal laughed, slapping his arm. "You're so full of it." She tugged a teenage girl in beside her, who had blonde hair with blue streaks. "This is Cassie. She was about eight when you saw her last?"

Eli nodded. "Hi, Cas. You've grown up."

"I remember you," Cassie said. "You babysat me with Turner sometimes."

Eli smiled. "Yeah, I did. You and your baby brother."

Krystal put her arm over her son's shoulders, tugging him forward. "This is Anthony. He was only two when you left."

"Right, Anthony. Do you still enjoy eating Play-Doh?"

"Um."

"Just kidding," Eli said with a laugh. "You were going through a phase back then."

"I like building stuff out of Legos," Anthony offered shyly.

"Legos are awesome," Eli said. "Wish I had some here."

Turner spoke up from behind Eli. "You guys hungry? Dinner's ready."

Turner and Eli were pressed into service after dinner, each lugging a box of holiday décor into the living room and placing it near the tree. Molly knelt on the floor so she could sort. Coach was in his recliner with an icepack on his knee, and Krystal and the kids were holding down the sofa, Anthony fidgeting impatiently and Cassie looking bored.

"Turner, will you do the lights while I get organized?" Molly asked, holding out a tangled strand of bulbs.

"I can do that," Eli offered.

"Sorry, hon. I've gotten used to calling on Turner." She turned, extending the cords to him.

While Eli worked to unknot the cords, Turner chuckled. "You could have dodged a bullet there," he said.

Eli shrugged, looking tense. Turner picked up the untangled end of the strand of twinkly lights, helping Eli keep it out of the way as he unwound the rest. "You know it's just habit like she said," Turner said in a low voice. "It's not a preference."

Eli looked up, dark eyes gleaming. "Sometimes ..."

"What?"

Eli stood up, taking the lights with him to an outlet farther from his mother. It put them within earshot of Krystal, but she was preoccupied with her restless son. Turner followed, waiting quietly, as Eli plugged in the lights to make sure all the bulbs were working.

As the white bulbs lit up, lighting his face from beneath, Eli said, "I chose to stay away. But sometimes it feels like they just replaced me." He looked up. "With you."

Turner's heart clenched. "Eli, no. Of course they didn't."

"They lean on you," Eli said. "They rely on you the way they should have been relying on me. And I know that's partly my fault ..."

Turner wanted desperately to hug Eli, but he couldn't. They weren't at that stage of their tentative friendship yet, and he didn't want to draw any undue attention. He had to make do with words, which had never been his strong suit.

"Eli, you don't need to feel guilty. Or jealous. I'm not sure what you're feeling."

"I feel out of place here."

Turner shook his head. "There's always a place for you here."

"In my parents' house? That hasn't always been true."

"There's always a place here for you," Turner repeated. "In Juniper, in your parents' house, with me."

"With you?"

"We grew up together. Our friendship was everything, and I know we hit a rough patch. But I want that back. Don't you?"

Eli nodded. "Yeah. I do."

Turner smiled, his heart aching. "Good. So, let's get these lights on the tree. It'll go faster if we do it together."

Eli exhaled slowly. "Yeah, you're right. I'm being silly."

"You're acclimating. Before you know it, it'll feel like home again," Turner said. "You won't want to leave."

Eli snorted. "Let's not get ahead of ourselves."

Eli's mom drew out delicate glass ornaments in gold, silver and white, along with a selection of angels she'd collected over the years. He needed to get back to the Waits tree farm and pick her up a gift. He hadn't done any Christmas shopping yet.

"Those are new," Eli said.

"Hmm?" His mother looked up from the ornaments she was handing out. "Yes. Once we had no little ones in the house it seemed like a good time to dress up the tree a bit."

As they each — with the exception of Coach — selected ornaments and hung them on the tree, Turner held up an old popsicle ornament with a picture of the two of them together at age six.

Eli moved over to his side, taking it from him. "I'm glad to see our ornament survived considering Mom decided to get all classy and buy pretty ornaments."

Turner grinned. "As if she'd ever throw anything away."

"What are you two gossiping about?" Krystal asked.

Turner showed her the ornament, and she took it, grinning. "You two were the cutest. So inseparable. We have a ton of these on my tree at home. Mom gave them to me because she doesn't put up a tree anymore. Not since Dad ..."

She trailed off, and Turner drew her in for one-armed hug. "I miss him too."

"Yeah," she said, forcing a smile. "But he'd want us to be happy on the holidays."

Eli turned his gaze to his father. "You must have thought I was a selfish brat, staying away. Wasting the time I had with my father when you'd lost yours. If that had been Coach..."

"Oh, Eli. We don't think that," Krystal said. "Still, I'm really glad you're here. Maybe you'll get a chance to mend fences with your dad?"

"I'm trying," Eli murmured, picking up another ornament. "We both are."

8

December 15th

Turner rolled up to Eli's house an hour before they were set to meet Cam for drinks Saturday night. It was a miracle he'd lasted that long; he'd been antsy all day. He hadn't had a reason to check in on the Harps, but Eli had been on his mind constantly since Thursday evening.

The visit to the tree farm and Christmas dinner had begun to break down the wall between him and Eli. But they hadn't really dealt with what pushed them apart in the first place, and he was afraid that once they did, Eli would shut down again. He would have to tread carefully when they ventured down that particular stretch of memory lane.

Eli came out of the house, taking the steps two at a time. He wore the fleece pullover Turner had lent him, along with the stocking cap pulled low to cover his ears. Only a few strands of dark brown hair peeked out at his temples. Tight, black jeans clung to his legs and made them seem even longer than usual. Turner didn't have to see his ass to know that it was going to be a distraction all night.

"Thank fuck you're here," Eli said as he slipped into the car. "Mom was driving me crazy."

"Really? I figured it'd be your dad giving you fits."

Eli buckled his seat belt, his movements sending the smell of an earthy cologne with hints of spice and citrus through the car. "Nah, I took him to his first day of therapy yesterday, and it wiped him out. They wanted to get him in a couple of times and give him some exercises to do at home, but then he'll be on his own all of Christmas week. I think he's secretly relieved, even though it'll set back his recovery time."

"Physical therapy is no joke," Turner said as he reversed his Jeep out of the driveway. "I had IT Band syndrome, basically from running too much and too hard on less than ideal terrain. I didn't have to have surgery, so it wasn't even in the same ballpark as what Coach is going through, and it was still painful as hell."

"What is that?" Eli asked, looking alarmed. "Are you better now?"

Turner warmed at Eli's concern. "Yeah, it's fine. I don't want to bore you with all the details. I had knee pain, so I had to do a few weeks of physical therapy exercises, along with icing and resting it. And I had to learn to pace myself. Running is a bit of an addiction for me."

"I'll never understand that," Eli said.

"You've never given it a chance," Turner said with a shrug. "Running, once your body adapts to the pace, can be really therapeutic. You should come out with me while you're here."

"Stop trying to get me hooked on your drug!" Eli joked.

Turner smirked. "But it's so good. You're not gonna believe how great it makes you feel." He winked, then went on more seriously. "I still have to remind myself not to overdo it. Taking Scout helps, because I don't want to exhaust him. Even though he has so much energy, and could probably keep up, I also know he'd run himself half to death, and I'd be responsible."

"Turner," Eli scolded, "don't you think you should care about yourself as much as you care about your dog?"

Turner pulled into the small parking lot in front of one of only two bars in Juniper. The Pine Nut Tavern was the more upscale of the two, with a large selection of wines and a piano tinkling in the background. Bubba's Pub was the other — a small, squat building that was dark inside and served cheap beer by the pitcher. If you weren't a snob or over the age of thirty-five, you went to Bubba's.

Turner cut the engine and answered Eli's question. "Look, I care about myself. But sometimes I'm better at thinking about other people's needs than my own."

"You always had such a big heart."

"There you go talking of about my big organs again," Turner said playfully. "Are you sure it's my heart you're interested in?"

Eli spluttered, his entire face flaming red. Turner wasn't sure he'd ever seen someone blush that hard.

"I don't think— I'm not ... I mean, I know when we— But that was ages go!"

Eli was clearly thrown by Turner's flirtation. What's more — if Turner was interpreting Eli's nearly incoherent words correctly — Eli was trying to say his crush was ages ago and long gone.

Which was good, really. Because they were going to be friends. And when Eli inevitably returned to California, Turner would follow him on Facebook and exchange messages and be happy to be a part of his life again.

"It was just a joke," Turner said lamely. "A bad one, obviously. Sorry."

Eli opened his car door and got out. In the cool night air, his blush cooled quickly. "Well, now that I've made an ass of myself, want to go in?" Eli asked.

Turner met him in front of the car. "I'm the ass. But sure, I think a couple of beers will take the edge off."

As soon as they stepped inside, Eli drew attention. He hadn't been to Juniper in eight years, and there were a few people their age in the bar. Tim Carrow was one of the first to notice them. He grinned wide. "Holy shit! Eli Harp. You look the same as ever."

Tim did not. For one thing, his hair was cut much shorter and worn in a conservative style, and a polo had replaced the sporty muscle tanks and T-shirts he'd favored in high school. He looked less imposing than he had as a teenager. He'd been a football player, a huge asshole to Eli and only marginally nicer to Turner. Now, he worked a desk job at a bank, like his father.

"Hey," Eli said.

"I'm Tim," he said. "One of the defensive linebackers."

Eli sucked in a breath. Turner was prepared to step forward and tell Tim to fuck off, but Eli beat him to the punch. "I remember. You were one of the unimpressive douche bags who couldn't get our team to the playoffs, right? I seem to remember you calling me names in the hallway. Really creative ones, like cocksucker."

"Oh, hey—"

"It's okay, Tim. You were right." Eli winked. "I like to suck cock. Maybe I'll even suck off Turner later tonight," he said, turning to Turner innocently when he choked on his own saliva. "What do you say, Turner? I know you're straight, but I just can't resist a cock. And I bet you've got a huge one."

Holy crap. Eli still thought he was straight? Turner had expected Molly Harp to pass on the news when he came out three years ago.

"As if you didn't suck his cock all through high school," Tim retorted. "We all know there's nothing straight about Turner."

Eli didn't so much as blink at Tim's claim, probably because his high school bullies had suggested Turner must be a gay, too, since he was Eli's friend. And once you cry wolf so many times ...

Turner produced a weak chuckle. "Well, I've never had any complaints either way."

"That's probably more than Tim can say," Eli said.

Tim spluttered. "There's nothing small about my cock," he said. He fumbled for his jeans button. "I'll prove it."

"Whoa, you sure you wanna show me? I might not be able to resist. I might fall to my knees right here."

Tim's eyes widened, and he looked a mix of disturbed and intrigued. "Would you really?"

"No, you dipshit," Turner spoke up. "He's yanking your chain. Just because he's gay doesn't mean he'll go for any cock shoved in his face."

"I guess you would know," Tim grumbled before turning away. Then he paused. "But hey, if you move back, we do mortgage lending at the bank. You can ask for me."

"Jesus fucking Christ," Eli said as Tim ambled over to someone else. "Was he for real?"

"Turns out that when you're in banking, sexuality matters less than money," Turner said.

"Go figure."

Turner stepped up to the bar to grab a pitcher of beer, and when he turned back with the pitcher and two cups, he saw Janine Little talking to Eli, gesturing wildly with her hands and pulling him into a big hug. Turner remembered that Janine had become Eli's de facto best friend the last half of senior year and felt a spark of jealousy.

"So, you're pregnant in a bar," Eli said just as Turner stepped up beside him. "What's that about?"

Janine rolled her eyes. "I'm not drinking. I'm the designated driver for Becca. She's home for the holidays and looking to get wasted. I think tensions at home are running a bit high." She leaned in closer, lowering her voice. "She's dating a guy in prison."

"What?"

"Swear to God. She saw some interview with him and started writing letters."

"No!"

"Yes!" Janine laughed. "I shouldn't judge. To each their own, right?" She glanced over at Turner. "What are you two up to?"

"Just catching up," Turner answered. "Cam is coming by soon."

"Really?" Janine said, her eyebrow hitching up. "That's interesting."

"Why is that interesting?" Eli asked. "I mean, I know we weren't really friends in high school, but he seems cool."

"Oh, no. He's cool." She glanced at Turner. "Right, Turner? You know him better than I do."

Turner cleared his throat. There was a landmine he needed to navigate around carefully. "Uh, yeah. Cam's a good guy. Hey, let's grab that table by the darts. Cam will want to play."

Eli nodded. "Sure. See you later, Janine."

Turner fidgeted when they sat down, drumming his fingers on the table and looking around the room. Eli poured them each a beer while he waited to find out what had Turner so wound up. Sliding the pint glass of pale ale across the table to Turner, he said, "You look like you need this."

"Yeah," Turner said, lifting the glass to take a long drink. He wiped at the foam on his upper lip, then finally met Eli's eyes.

"It occurs to me that I should probably tell you something."

"Okay?"

"I kind of figured you'd already heard it through the grapevine, but now I'm thinking I was wrong."

"Is this about Cam?"

"No," Turner said. Then his forehead wrinkled. "Well, kind of."

"I haven't exactly been plugged into Juniper's gossip mill, but I figured Cam was into men," Eli said. "Unless my gaydar is broken?"

"Your gaydar isn't broken," Turner said. He drummed his fingers on the table again. "Thing is, Cam isn't the only one—"

"Hey, guys! Talking about me already?" Cam strolled up, interrupting Turner. "All good things I hope?"

He wore jeans, work boots, and a flannel shirt over a muscle tank. His biceps strained the sleeves, which he'd rolled up to his forearms for good measure. Cam's arms were the most built part of his body from all the work he did out on the farm, and he knew it. He'd dressed to impress, and Turner knew Cam had no interest in rekindling a romance with him. *Just great.*

Eli grinned, unaware of the tension gathering in Turner's body. "I usually have to know a guy more than a day to trash talk him."

Well, fuck.

For a coming out speech, that was a major fail. One was usually supposed to actually *come out* in these situations.

Turner didn't have a lot of experience in how best to tell your friend that you were actually into guys after all. Turner hadn't really *come out* much, even when he did give up the closet. He'd started dating Cam and let everyone work it out for themselves. But that wasn't an option now. And clearly Eli really had *not* heard through the grapevine, or he would have figured out what Turner was trying to tell him.

Unless he considered it old news? Maybe he was more interested in Cam's sexuality because he actually wanted to hook up with Turner's ex? That would put the fucking cherry on top of this shit sundae.

Turner tuned in to the conversation in time to hear Cam ask Eli if he was single. *He didn't waste any fucking time, did he?*

Eli smiled. "No boyfriend."

That meant Levi really was a roommate. Not that it mattered.

76

"Yeah? I'm single too. What are the odds?" Cam said with a grin.

Eli laughed. "I don't know about you, but the odds are always pretty good I'll be single."

"Ah, so you're not a relationship guy," Cam said as he swiped Turner's beer and took a big drink.

"Not by choice, really," Eli said. "I'm not afraid of commitment. I'm just really awful at dating. It's pretty much been a disaster from my very first crush."

His eyes met Turner's for a split second, just long enough for Turner to know Eli meant him, before he looked down at the table. Eli scratched at a rough edge on the wood tabletop.

"You hook up with any hot surfers?" Cam asked. "Or Silicon Valley nerds. You know, whatever floats your boat."

Eli chuckled. "Maybe a couple."

"Surfers or nerds?"

Eli raised an eyebrow. "Who says I can't do both?"

"Oh, ho," Cam said with a laugh. "You sound naughty. I like that in a man."

"Nah, I'm kidding. I've had some hookups, but usually I just attract bears, or worse, daddies. I have enough issues with my dad without going there."

Cam snorted. "Well, I'm a bear, but I promise not to be your daddy."

Eli laughed again, his cheeks flushing pink, and Turner kind of wanted to punch Cam in the face.

"Let's play darts," Turner suggested instead, standing without waiting for an answer.

He grabbed the darts from the ledge beneath the board and stepped back a few paces. When he looked over, Eli and Cam were continuing their conversation, their eyes on each other.

Irritated, Turner blew his first shot, catching the edge of the dartboard.

"Nice work," Cam said. "Are you trying to lose?"

Turner flipped him the bird. "Maybe I was distracted by your obnoxious flirting."

"Hey, can't blame a guy for trying," he said. "I bet I can flirt and still wipe the floor with you."

Turner fired off his second and third darts, scoring slightly better, before stalking forward to pull them out of the board.

"I'm pretty awful at darts," Eli said, "so if anyone's going to lose…"

"I'll give you some tips," Cam offered.

Turner held up the darts in his hand. "Or Eli could just come give it a shot without you hanging all over him," he suggested.

Eli walked over and took the darts from his hand. "Way to be an asshole."

"I think you've got some drool on you," Turner replied, brushing at his shoulder.

"Lighten up, Turner. Flirting's fun. You should try it sometime."

Turner let his fingers drag down Eli's arm as he dropped his hand. "Yeah? You gonna give me lessons?"

Their eyes caught and held for a long moment. Then Eli looked down, his lashes fanning across his cheeks, and bit his bottom lip. Fuck, but he was sexy.

"I wouldn't presume," Eli murmured.

Turner's blood heated, and he wanted nothing more than Eli to presume his body was a tree for him to climb, but that wasn't happening.

Cam's voice boomed out. "Sometime today, guys!"

Eli startled at Cam's words, turning to throw the dart without aiming properly. His shaky hand didn't help matters, and the dart thunked into the wall beside the dartboard.

"Shoot," he said weakly. "Told you I was bad at this."

Turner had thoroughly unnerved him. What was with all the touching and eye contact and suggestive tone? If he didn't know better, he'd think Turner was attracted to him. But it had to be his imagination.

"You just need to aim," Cam suggested. "And maybe tell Turner to fuck off so you can focus."

"You better listen to Daddy," Turner taunted.

"Fuck off," Eli said with a laugh.

Turner grinned, backing up a few steps to give him space. "Already such a good boy."

Eli rolled his eyes, turning back to face the board and raising the dart.

"What's wrong, Turner, you jealous?" Cam taunted. "You want to be my boy again?"

His boy? What the fuck?

"Cam," Turner said in a warning tone. "Shut up."

Eli was frozen, the dart still in his hand. He should throw it, but his heart was racing, and he was trying to make sense of this weird exchange as pieces clicked into place. The picture wasn't fully formed, but he was getting there.

"Aw, don't be that way," Cam teased. "I know you're hot for Eli. I'm just pushing your buttons."

"Goddamn it," Turner swore. "He doesn't know—"

Eli whirled. "You're *gay?*"

The dart, completely forgotten, flew from his fingers as he turned. It whizzed through the air, a straighter shot than he'd managed when throwing at the dartboard, and hit its unintended target.

Turner Williams. The closeted, lying, gorgeous man who had broken his heart in high school.

"Oh shit," Cam exclaimed.

Turner didn't make a sound. Eyes wide, he looked down at the dart still quivering as it jutted out of the tender flesh just above his armpit. God, those dart tips weren't too long, were they? Eli didn't actually *hurt* him?

Clenching his jaw, Turner tugged out the dart. Immediately, a small dot of blood seeped through his T-shirt. Turner lifted a hand, pressing it against the tiny wound.

"Fuck, that stings."

Eli stared at him, torn between horrified embarrassment and righteous anger. "Are you okay?"

"I'll live," Turner said. Tossing the dart on the table, he grimaced. "I suppose I deserved that for telling you while you were armed with sharp things."

"You haven't told me anything, actually," Eli pointed out. "Are you really ..."

Turner looked him square in the eye. "I'm bisexual."

Boom. It was as if a bomb went off inside his body. Eli closed his eyes as he fought down the emotions that threatened to overwhelm him. Turner wasn't straight. Turner had never told him, hadn't *trusted* him.

When he opened them again, Turner had closed the gap and stood inches from him.

"I was trying to tell you when Cam got here," he said. "I'm sorry you found out like this. I honestly thought your mom had told you. I wasn't trying to hide anything."

"Not now, you mean." When Turner looked confused, he added, "You weren't trying to hide it now. But what about then? Did you know before I left?"

"Yeah," Turner said roughly.

"And that night?"

Eli didn't need to explain what night. The mistletoe kiss had become an infamous event in their lives. It was the breaking point for their friendship and Eli's unrequited attraction. Which was hard enough to take when he'd believed Turner was straight, but now that he knew Turner just didn't *want* him? It was ten times worse.

Turner nodded, his face filled with regret.

Eli spun, throwing the third dart he still held hard at the board. He hit it almost dead center. It was amazing how a little anger could really focus you.

Cam had been watching their exchange in a horrified silence. Now, he nudged Turner. "You should probably disinfect that."

Eli turned around, feeling a niggle of guilt when he saw the small bloodstain on Turner's shirt. "I didn't mean to do that," he said.

"I know. It's okay."

"I'm shit with coordination and clumsy to boot. You know that about me. I'd never—"

He broke off as Turner took his hands in his, squeezing. "Eli, it's okay. It was an accident. Besides, it's just a tiny prick."

"Unlike you," Eli muttered.

Turner laughed weakly. "Are you calling me a huge prick?"

Eli's gaze met his. "Seems fitting."

Cam cleared his throat. "So, uh, I'm sorry for running my mouth. I think maybe I should take off and let you guys talk."

Eli pulled away from Turner, crossing his arms over his chest. "Clearly Turner doesn't talk about important things. But calling it a night seems like a good idea."

Turner sighed. "I'll take you home."

As Eli tugged on his borrowed fleece, Cam put his hand on Turner's arm. "I'm sorry. You're out, so I just assumed ..."

"Not your fault," Turner muttered. "I can't blame anyone but myself."

9

Once they were out of Cam's company, Eli went icy cold again. And silent.

Turner knew they should talk about it, but Eli was right — he *was* shitty at that sort of thing. Which was how he'd ended up in this situation. But even he knew that they couldn't move forward as friends if they didn't deal with the past.

"Are you pissed that I didn't come out in high school or that I didn't kiss you back?"

That was the wrong thing to say.

"Fuck you, Turner. Fuck. You!"

Turner gripped the steering wheel tighter. Shit, he was messing this up. He meant that to be a genuine question, but it sounded more like an accusation.

"That came out wrong. I didn't mean for that to sound like ..." He shook his head. "I was an idiot that night. Seriously."

Eli scoffed. "Yeah, okay."

"Eli—"

"Just shut up, okay? I don't want to talk about it. You're bi. Good for you. Just take me home."

Turner clenched his teeth so hard his jaw ached. He'd epically fucked up. He could feel the waves of hurt and anger coming off Eli in the interior of the Jeep. If he didn't do something, he was going to lose his friend all over again.

He drove in silence, tension thick between them, until the Jeep's headlights flashed across the Harps' dark lawn then swung over the front of the house as he turned into the driveway. Eli had his hand on the door handle before Turner had even shifted into park.

"Thanks for the ride."

Turner clamped a hand down on Eli's thigh. "Please don't run away again."

Eli's leg tensed, and Turner immediately pulled his hand back. "You think I run away from my problems, is that it?"

"Maybe," Turner said cautiously. He was walking on thin ice already, and Eli looked like one push would make him explode into a thousand pieces.

"You ran first," he said quietly. "I might have left Juniper, but you left me."

"No, I—"

"You ran straight into Kara Whitmore's lips! I saw you making out with her the same night you rejected me. I thought it was because you were straight. But you *weren't* straight."

"I'm sorry—"

Eli wasn't done. He kept speaking as if he hadn't even heard Turner.

"You weren't straight, which means you just didn't want me," Eli continued. "And you should have been man enough to tell me the truth!"

Turner waited a beat to see if Eli was going to keep going, but he fell quiet, breathing hard. It was dark in the car, too dark to see, and Turner clicked on the dome light. Eli's face — and every bit of vulnerability in his expression — was suddenly illuminated. He squinted, looking down, as the soft light washed over him.

"That's what you think," Turner said, "that I didn't *want* you?"

"What else would I think?" he asked flatly.

Turner unbuckled his seat belt and leaned over, raising a hand to Eli's face. Gently, he brushed a thumb along his jawline. "You should think I was a coward and a fool," he said. "But never that. Because that would be a huge lie."

Eli raised his eyes to Turner's. "What are you saying?"

"You were everything to me," Turner said. "But I hadn't figured out how to be me yet. I was afraid and stupid."

Turner's thumb drifted to Eli's bottom lip that he so often bit when nervous. He pulled it gently from Eli's teeth, then brushed the pad of his thumb over soft skin. Eli breathed out unsteadily.

"You were scared?" he asked in a hopeful tone. Like he wanted so much to understand and give Turner a pass. Turner knew he didn't really deserve that easy forgiveness, but if Eli granted it, he'd take it. Because he couldn't bear the thought of being iced out again.

"You were already out, and it was horrible," Turner said. "Coach made you miserable. The kids at school were shitheads. I didn't want to be a target too."

"But people already gave you hell for being my friend," Eli said, sounding confused.

"That was different," Turner said quietly. "I could play the hero." He snorted. "I was nothing but a scared little boy who wanted to be your protector. Coming out would have ruined that. It sounds so fucking selfish and dumb when I say it out loud."

Eli sat back, appearing to think that over, and Turner reluctantly dropped his hand. Somehow, it crept onto Eli's knee, squeezing gently. It wasn't sexual, but Turner needed the connection to Eli. Maybe partly from a fear he'd flee the car any second.

"It was a confusing time for me too," Eli finally said. "Everyone has to come out in their own time. I have no right to be angry, not really."

Turner shook his head. "You can be as mad as you want."

Eli sighed. "I'm not mad. I am a little sad you didn't trust me.

I would have kept your secret." He paused. "And if what you say is true, about ... um, being into me, we could have comforted each other."

"With our lips?" Turner teased.

"Lips. Dicks," Eli said with a smirk. "The works."

"Jesus Christ, I wanted to kiss you so much. You have no idea," Turner blurted. "I still do."

Eli's eyes went wide. His tongue came out to moisten his lips. "You don't really mean that."

"Oh, I really fucking do." Turner leaned in slowly. "Give me a do-over? Just one kiss to show you how I really felt then and now."

Eli blinked, his lips parting.

Daring to hope Eli might give him this, after everything — that he might forgive Turner for hiding a part of himself, for being too afraid to deal with half the shit Eli did, for pushing him away — Turner's heart beat so hard he nearly didn't hear the words when Eli whispered them.

"Kiss me then, Turner."

Eli couldn't breathe. Couldn't think. Somehow, he managed to answer Turner, his words a breathy whisper that ordinarily would have embarrassed him. But Turner didn't hesitate to turn words to action.

Turner kissed him, and Eli's heart exploded into a frantic pace. Turner's lips were on his, *finally*. And all his anger, all his disappointment washed away on a wave of endorphins.

This felt right. It was as if he'd been holding his breath for eight years, and he could finally exhale.

But it was over too soon. Eli hadn't gotten a taste of Turner's tongue, the kiss quick and chaste. He hadn't gotten to run his fingers through his hair. Hadn't put his hands on him at all.

Nothing but their lips had touched, and it was the single, best kiss of his life.

"I'd like us to be friends again, real friends," Turner said. "Even after you leave again for California."

Oh, right. Eli would be leaving. Turner would be staying. Nothing had changed.

His racing heart slowed. Grew heavy. Thudded hollowly.

"Friends," he repeated.

"I know you're not staying long," Turner added. "So, it's just a kiss. Between friends."

"A friendly kiss," Eli said.

Turner chuckled. "Yeah."

"Okay," Eli said.

And yet he sensed something more between the lines of Turner's spoken words. Honesty, yes, but also yearning. Could it be possible that Turner wanted him as much as he'd always wanted Turner?

There was only one way to find out.

Eli wrapped a hand around the back of Turner's neck, tugged him close, and kissed him hard. If he was only getting one kiss, he was going to make it count. He was going to kiss the daylights out of Turner and decide for himself how much Turner Williams wanted Elijah Harp.

Turner gasped in surprise as Eli brushed his tongue along his bottom lip, coaxing him to come out and play. With a groan, Turner parted his lips and met Eli's tongue with his own. While they kissed, Eli ran his hands into Turner's hair, trying to memorize every sensation. But it was difficult to absorb the details — the surprising softness of Turner's hard mouth against his, the tickle of his short beard against Eli's face, the silkiness of Turner's hair under his fingers at last — when his body was overwhelmed with hormones and adrenaline, his heart racing and lust firing in his veins.

Turner made delicious low rumbles of pleasure in his chest as

Eli toyed with his tongue, bringing out all his skill to make this kiss the most memorable Turner would ever have. Turner's hands cradled his face, big enough to cover his cheeks. With winter coats on, the kiss couldn't go any further, as much as Eli would love to feel Turner's body. His cock didn't know that, and it thudded in complaint in his jeans.

After what seemed a lifetime — and also the blink of an eye — they broke for air.

"Jesus, Eli," Turner growled, his voice hoarse and sexy as hell.

Eli smiled, unrepentant. "Just being friendly."

With Turner gaping, his chest still heaving, Eli unbuckled his seat belt and popped open the car door, sliding out.

Turner stared after him, his lips red and damp from the kissing.

"It's late," Eli said. "You better get home to Scout. Don't forget to disinfect your shoulder."

He moved to shut the door, and Turner found his voice. "Wait, Eli!"

Eli ducked his head down to meet Turner's eyes. "Yeah?"

"We're okay, right?" Turner asked.

Eli nodded. He didn't necessarily like the choices Turner had made, but they were both kids. Eli knew better than anyone that Juniper had been a shitty place to be out and proud. If he'd seen someone going through hell, maybe he would have stayed hidden in the closet too.

"We're good," he said, meaning it, as he turned to go inside.

He wouldn't condemn Turner for a highly personal decision made in a stressful time. He realized, when he thought about it, that he'd never actually told Turner how he felt. He'd tried to kiss him, in a hallway where they could have been seen, and used mistletoe as a convenient excuse. Maybe, if he'd been braver and talked honestly, Turner would have done the same.

It was all water under the bridge now. All they could do was start again and try to rebuild a friendship.

If that was Eli's one and only kiss with Turner, it had been a good one. He had no regrets. But something told him it wouldn't be. Eli hoped so anyway. Because Turner Williams had been all Eli had ever wanted for Christmas. And eight years later than planned was still better than never.

10

December 16th

Doggy breath and whines dragged Turner from sleep. Scout's face was so close to his, Turner reared back, startled.

"Good morning to you too," he rasped.

Scout whined in response, rubbing his face on the bed beside Turner. Well, he needed to wash the sheets anyway.

He scratched Scout behind the ears. "Okay, I'm awake now." He pointed toward the floor. "Get down."

Scout obeyed after shooting him one last pleading look, and Turner sat up against the headboard and reached for his phone. It was Sunday, so he didn't need to be at school, but generally he was an early riser. Partly because Scout wouldn't have it any other way and partly because his internal clock didn't understand that weekends were any different from schooldays.

He was surprised to see it was seven a.m., a full two hours later than he usually slept.

"Damn." He rubbed a hand over his face. No wonder Scout was antsy. As if on cue, Scout yipped from the doorway.

"Okay, I'm getting up," he said, rolling out of bed and yanking open a dresser drawer for his running clothes.

Turner had slept soundly the night before — once he got to sleep. It had taken some time, wound up as he was by that kiss with Eli. He kept replaying it on a loop, wondering what might have happened next in different circumstances. Would Eli have come home with him, if he'd asked? Gotten naked with him?

Hard and horny, Turner slipped into the bathroom without Scout to take care of his problem. He shouldn't have kissed Eli if he didn't want anything but friendship. He realized that now. But Eli had looked so vulnerable, so hurt by Turner's past rejection. He'd wanted to show Eli that he cared, that he'd always cared, to erase a little of his pain.

Right, that's why. Not because you've been imagining his lips against yours since the moment you saw him again.

Turner truly had meant to keep it a sweet, chaste kiss. He hadn't banked on Eli taking it to hot and steamy. Eli was bolder than he was, always had been. And God, he'd kissed perfectly. Turner closed his eyes and tried to remember the exact feel of Eli's tongue stroking his as he fisted his cock and squeezed. The details were elusive, already fading in intensity. He huffed in frustration, stroking his cock harder, and let his fantasies unspool instead. Eli in his house. Eli on his knees, looking up through those dark lashes of his. Eli licking the tip of his cock, then sucking him down.

Turner came with a grunt into the toilet. Opening his eyes, he grimaced. Yeah, that was sexy. Unsatisfying orgasm achieved, he set about his morning routine, and before long, he and Scout were pulling up to the Harps' house.

With Eli in town, they'd be unlikely to need anything from him, but Turner couldn't resist the opportunity to exchange a few words with Eli. Maybe get a sense of what he was thinking or feeling after the night before. Not just about the kiss, but everything Turner had unloaded on him. Now that Eli had slept on it, he might be less forgiving. It was a hell of a lot to process.

Scout ran ahead to the door, happy to visit the Harps even though it delayed his morning run. Turner slipped inside, wiped Scouts' feet, and then they both headed toward the kitchen and the scent of coffee.

Molly and Coach sat at the little kitchenette table, sipping coffee. Two mostly empty plates were piled between them. The Harps generally didn't use the dining room except for more formal meals.

Scout's nails clicked on the tile, drawing their attention. Coach held out a bit of leftover bacon for Scout to snatch up, and then scratched him on the head, while Molly greeted Turner. "Well, this is a surprise! I didn't think we'd see you on a Sunday."

Turner hesitated, taking in Molly's dress. He'd forgotten the Harps usually went to church on Sunday mornings. "Just habit, I guess. I wasn't thinking about the day of the week."

"Do you want something? Coffee?"

"No, I just stopped by to say good morning and to make sure Coach was still recovering well."

"It was a knee replacement," Coach grumbled. "I'm doing fine, except my physical therapist is obviously a sadist. Not only does he get to torture me at the therapy center, but he gave me exercises so I can torture myself when I'm home."

Turner smirked. "You did say you planned to recover fully in half the recommended time. No pain, no gain."

"I'm familiar with the cliché. Thanks, Turner."

Turner chuckled. "You're a tough nut. You've got this. Just don't overdo it. That might slow your recovery down."

"Heaven help us then," Molly said. "I've never seen my husband in such a rotten mood. He needs to get back work."

When a lull fell in the conversation, Turner shifted awkwardly. "No Eli this morning?"

Molly smiled at him, something knowing in her expression. "He's still sleeping. You must have kept him out late."

Not really. But perhaps Eli had just as much trouble getting to sleep as he had. Turner only hoped it was for the same reasons.

"Well, I can see it's a church day. I'll just hit your bathroom, if that's all right, and be on my way. Scout is anxious for his run."

"Sure," Molly said. "There's no rush. Coach is staying home. He's not really up for navigating the church steps just yet."

Turner went down the hall, then stopped outside Eli's bedroom. The door wasn't fully latched, and he couldn't resist pushing it open to peek inside.

Eli was sacked out, deep asleep by the looks of it. He lay on his stomach, the blankets pushed down to his waist, and the full expanse of his bare back was exposed. His hair was sticking out in three directions, and his face was mashed into the pillow, but Turner thought it might be the sexiest sight he'd ever seen.

Friends, my ass. How am I supposed to resist that?

Turner drank his fill, then eased the door closed, and returned to the kitchen to say his good-byes and go run off his sexual frustration.

———

Eli met Janine at a coffee shop downtown around ten a.m. Most the snow had melted off, and finally he could drive somewhere without embarrassing himself.

She enveloped him in a big hug just inside the front door. "Thanks for meeting me. I wanted to catch up, and it wasn't going to happen while I was on babysitting duty. And I don't mean this one," she added, patting her round tummy.

Eli chuckled. Janine made a cute mommy-to-be, all slender limbs and a tight, round belly. Her skin glowed with health. Eli had never understood that expression about pregnant women glowing, but he got it now.

"How is your friend?"

"Hungover," Janine said. "And still crazy about her inmate boyfriend." She shrugged. "Who am I to judge? I married Gary Wassel. Plenty of people thought I was nuts."

They moved into line, chatting as they waited to order drinks. When Eli got to the front, he ordered a nonfat vanilla latte with sugar-free syrup.

Janine looked him over. "Are you kidding?"

"What?"

"You've barely got an ass! Why are you ordering nonfat?"

Eli shook his head. "I pretty much never exercise. This is my penance."

Janine rolled her eyes. "That is a pointless waste." She turned to the barista. "I'll take a peppermint mocha with all the fat and sugar, as any sane person should during the holiday season."

The barista, a petite brunette with a spray of freckles and a friendly smile, laughed. "You want whipped cream?"

"Does a pregnant woman crave pickles?"

"Um..."

"The answer is 'yes.' No, the answer is, 'Hell yes, I want whipped cream.' If you leave it off, I might have to hurt you."

The barista's eyes widened, and Eli tugged Janine back from the counter with a laugh. "Those pregnancy hormones are something, huh? Why don't you go ahead and add extra whipped cream to be safe?"

"Yeah, I want extra!" Janine called as the young woman scurried away without charging them.

"You scared her."

Janine snorted. "Oops. Being pregnant comes with a kind of power. You can get away with all kinds of stuff. It's gone to my head."

The brunette — her nametag read Angie — returned with a tall cup heaped high with whipped cream. "Here's your peppermint mocha."

She began to ring up the drinks.

"What about mine?" Eli asked.

"Oh, they'll call you when it's done. I didn't want to keep Mommy here waiting."

"See?" Janine said as they found their way to seats. "Power."

They settled on a low sofa because Janine said trying to sit on one of the tall, hard stools at the counter would make her feel like a cherry tomato on a toothpick. She hadn't yet reached the massive stage of pregnancy, but you wouldn't know it by the way she talked.

"Okay, tell me about your boys' night. You left pretty early."

Eli pondered what to tell her, then went for funny. "You didn't see me nail Turner with a dart?"

"You didn't!"

"Yep," Eli said. "Bull's eye."

Janine giggled. "Oh my God, I shouldn't laugh. I like Turner. I did think it was a little weird he and Cam were hanging out."

Eli nodded. "Because they're exes?"

She blew out a breath. "So you know. That's a relief. I was worried I was going to have to be the messenger of awkward news."

"Eli!" a low voice called from the counter. Eli popped up, happy to have a minute away from the conversation, and went to grab his vanilla latte. Taking a sip, he sighed happily. It was delicious even without fat and sugar, thank you very much.

When he returned to the sofa, Janine occupied herself drinking until he decided to answer. "I didn't know before last night."

Her eyebrows went up, but she didn't speak.

"I didn't even know he was bi."

"He's been out for a long time. He and Cam broke up at least two years ago, and they dated for a while."

Eli smiled wryly. "I wasn't exactly in the loop."

She nudged him. "Yeah, I noticed. If you'd stayed in touch, I could have told you."

"Sorry. College was kind of consuming, you know? And without coming back for holidays, my life in Juniper felt really far away."

"I get it."

"Yeah?"

"No, not really. I only went to community college nearby. Took some art classes. I hold a wine-and-paint thing once a month. You should come if you're ever here again."

"Sounds fun."

"You can bring a date," she said. "Maybe Turner?"

"Stop fishing."

She laughed. "Fine, are you ready to get your Christmas shopping done?"

"Yeah. I hate Christmas shopping, but it beats hanging out with my parents all day. Dad would probably have me cleaning the garage for him by now." He gave a shudder. "Or watching NFL Network."

Eli was driving home when his phone rang. Expecting another call from Barb asking for a family update — or even an official eviction notice from Levi now that his girlfriend was moving into the apartment — Eli answered without checking the caller ID. "Yo!"

Turner chuckled, his low rumble sending warmth through Eli. "Hey, Eli."

Eli cradled the phone between his neck and shoulder so he could keep both hands on the steering wheel. "Hi."

A lengthy pause followed. Eli felt shy and uncertain of where they stood. Turner said he wanted to be friends, but words were cheap. The chemistry when they kissed, that was something that had never come easily to Eli. It was worth exploring, in his opin-ion. But he'd have to get Turner on the same page.

"You busy?" Turner asked.

"Just headed home. I did some Christmas shopping today."

"Oh yeah?" Turner said. "I did too. Had to take my niece and nephew. Surprised I didn't see you. You hit the mall?"

"We mostly stayed downtown," Eli said.

"That explains it. You too afraid to drive your tiny car any farther?" he teased.

"My car was just fine, thank you."

"For a convertible in winter."

Eli huffed. "It made more sense in California." Turner made a skeptical noise, egging him on. "It's always warm there!"

"Still not the safest thing to drive, Eli."

Annoyed, he said, "Like I told Cam last night, Daddies aren't my kink." While Turner spluttered, he went on, "Guys loved my car, by the way. I could put the top down on an isolated road and ride the biggest surfer right in my front seat."

"Jesus, Eli," Turner said in a strangled voice.

"What?" Eli asked innocently, as he flipped his blinker on and made the turn onto his block.

"You could have been arrested for indecency."

Eli laughed. "Sweet of you to worry, but I was careful."

"I just bet."

Oh, what was that delicious sound? Why, it was the sound of Eli Harp getting under Turner Williams' skin. *Excellent.*

Eli grinned evilly into the rearview mirror. "So, you were asking if I was busy?"

Turner cleared his throat. "Uh, yeah, I'm going running this evening with Scout. Thought you might want to join us. Finally see what the addiction is all about."

"Turner, don't you think I've seen plenty of you running junkies? My dad is a track coach."

"Just humor me," Turner said. "It's a low-key way for us to hang out and catch up as friends."

Eli considered that as he pulled the car into the garage and cut the engine. Running wasn't at all his thing, but he did want to spend time with Turner. It was kind of essential if he wanted to get another kiss, and hopefully more, out of his friend.

"Are you sure you wouldn't rather come over and watch a Christmas movie with me? Or, better yet, take me to a dark theater." Eli waggled his eyebrows, even though there was no one to see it. "We could sit in the back row and—"

"I've got school tomorrow," Turner said quickly. "Can't stay out late."

"Bummer."

"So, is that a no to running?" Turner's voice turned playful. "How else will I get you hooked on my drug of choice?"

Eli would much rather get hooked on another kind of pleasurable high. But before a great reward came great sacrifice. With that in mind, he reluctantly agreed.

"I'll go on one condition."

"What's that?"

"You hang out with me tomorrow night doing something of my choosing. And I know you have school all week, so we don't have to be out super late, okay? Just ... I wouldn't mind seeing the holiday light displays. We could go for a drive, right? That's safe enough."

Turner breathed evenly into the phone line. "I guess you're onto me then," he said. "I'm a little afraid of what might happen in a dark theater."

Eli exhaled slowly, waiting for his heart to calm. He didn't want Turner to know how damn giddy that made him. He needed to play this cool.

"Is that right?" he said innocently. "I didn't know you were afraid of the dark."

"Funny."

"So, is it a deal? We run tonight, and tomorrow, we cruise holiday lights?"

"Cruising with Eli. That sounds..."

"Good?"

Turner chuckled. "Too good, but yeah, it's a deal. I'll pick you up around five."

11

When Turner pulled up to the curb, Eli was in the front yard straining to set up a large piece of plywood. Turner immediately recognized it as one of the greeting cards the neighborhood was known for during the holiday season.

Turner opened the door for Scout, and the dog tore across the yard, tail wagging with excitement. Eli half turned, propping up the plywood, as Scout jumped up against his hip and made him stumble.

Turner hurried after Scout, happy for an excuse to rush across the grass so he didn't look too damn eager to see Eli. Even if he was. He grabbed Scout's collar and dragged him back. "Calm down," he said as Scout yipped again.

With his free hand, he pressed the other side of the plywood, helping Eli shove it back. There was a frame of sorts — sort of like a supersized card stand— and once Scout backed off Turner helped Eli get it set up.

"Thanks," Eli said, breathless. "It's not that heavy, but it's awkward."

"No problem. I could have helped you with this. Didn't think Coach was putting one out this year."

Eli's grimaced. "Yeah, he wasn't. I got this bright idea I should put it up for him. Prove I was capable of helping out."

"That seems nice," Turner said. "Why the face?"

"I did something."

Uh-oh. Turner remembered that expression. Eli had worn it the time he'd "borrowed" his dad's car without asking and ended up grounded for three weeks.

Eli stepped back and gestured down to the plywood.

Turner's eyes widened as he took it in. It was painted in stripes, starting with red, which made sense for Christmas, but then progressing through orange, yellow, green, blue and purple. It didn't really click, though, until Turner read the large stenciled words in the middle: MAKE THE YULETIDE GAY.

Eli had spelled out the words with tinsel and affixed a small spotlight just underneath them so they'd be readable at night. He'd also fastened a string of multicolored Christmas lights around the edge of the plywood, but with the context of his message and the rainbow colors he'd painted the plywood, there was no mistaking his intent.

It was the gay pride flag, with a little Christmas thrown on top.

"Wow," Turner said.

He put a hand over his mouth, not to hide his shock, but to cover his grin. Eli might be pushing it with Coach, but this was so Eli. At least, it was the Eli that Turner knew before he'd come out and been slowly ground under people's heels.

"I know," Eli groaned. "Why do I do these things? The whole point of doing this display was to prove to Coach I'm capable."

"Well, you've certainly done that," Turner said, unable to hide his amusement.

"I'm glad you find it funny. He's going to think I'm rebelling like a brat. I was supposed to leave all this acting out crap behind with my teenage years."

"So, why are you acting out? Coach do something?"

Eli shook his head. "That's just it. Coach has been trying really hard. It's like I was possessed when I was buying supplies. I went to that Main Street hardware store, and the owner was a total dick."

"Mike Kraft," Turner said with a nod. The old guy had run the store for their entire lifetime, and he'd been one of the few negative experiences Turner had while dating Cam. They'd gone in one time to get paint, and he'd made a snide comment. Turner had been sure never to go back. "Surely you knew he was an old homophobe from when you were in high school."

Eli sighed. "Guess I thought he wouldn't recognize me. Or that maybe, I don't know, he would have lightened up over the years. Wishful thinking."

"There's a hardware store out on Monroe Street. That's where I go."

Eli looked at him, surprised. "He was rude to you too?"

Turner hesitated, not wanting to worsen Eli's perception of Juniper, which already wasn't the best. "He was one of the few," he admitted. "Most people were fine with it. It really hasn't been the ordeal I expected it to be, especially considering I work at the school. In sports, no less."

"That is pretty surprising."

"It helps that I had Coach's support," Turner said. "And that our team was bringing home state medals."

Eli smirked. "You jocks always get all the breaks."

"Sorry."

"I'm glad my father did the right thing," Eli added.

"I wish he could have done the same for you."

Eli shrugged, looking back to his holiday display with anxiety. "Maybe if I didn't do this kind of shit, he would. I just can't seem to hold it in. When that old bastard gave me shit, I felt this need to assert my gayness."

Turner couldn't check a chuckle. "It's ... fucking genius."

"So I'm not insane?"

"Oh, you're certifiable," Turner said with a laugh.

Turner wasn't sure how Coach would react. He and Turner had more than a few talks about sexuality over the years. After Turner started dating Cam, everyone in Juniper found out he was bi, and Coach called him to the office. Turner was braced to fight for his job or his reputation or both, but Coach only wanted to understand.

He didn't. He was raised in the Bible Belt, and Turner had to talk him out of throwing out the trite "it's a sin" argument and really try to understand human sexuality. Coach finally came to a place where he could at least accept that Eli couldn't help who he was, and that he surely wouldn't have chosen to be gay when the price was his family and friends.

This little rebellion, though, might be too flashy for Coach. Eli might have been riled by Mike Kraft, but Turner thought maybe he was testing his father too. Trying to see just how accepting he really was.

"Time to face the music," Eli said morosely. "I'll get ready for that run before I tell him. At least with a bum knee, he can't chase me down."

"Look at you getting in the spirit of running already."

Eli flipped him the bird, making him laugh, as they headed for the front door. Turner whistled for Scout, pulling him from his snuffling exploration of the shrubbery around the corner of the house, and they went inside.

Eli went to his bedroom and tugged on his running clothes, frustrated he'd put himself in this position. He knew how much Coach loved to have a holiday display outside, and he'd gone into the project with the best of intentions. Yet, he'd still managed to sabotage himself.

When he was a kid, the holiday displays were a source of

tension between him and his father. He never seemed to do anything right. He didn't listen to his father's instructions closely enough and used the wrong tools, or he was too slow or too messy. It always ended up being a miserable experience.

Today was his chance to show Coach that he'd grown up and could do something right. He'd meant to do something nice, but Mike Kraft had pissed him off, and he'd ended up making a statement to all of Juniper instead of one to his father.

Fuck.

Dressed for a run, Eli couldn't delay anymore. He emerged from his bedroom and found Turner and Coach talking in the living room. "Where's Mom?" he asked, more to stall than because he needed to know.

"She went out for coffee with a friend," Coach said. "She's been cooped up too much lately because of me."

Eli nodded. "Yeah. She's practically chained to the stove."

Coach scowled. "You know your mom. She watches cooking shows and collects cookbooks like they're going out of style. It's not a chore to her."

"Yeah, I know," Eli said, not eager to start a new argument with Coach. He had to wonder if his mother didn't want something more out of life, but now wasn't the time to talk about it.

"Ready to run?" Turner asked.

"Yeah." Eli turned to Coach. "Um, I sort of set up a greeting card and lights display out front."

Coach straightened from his slump in the recliner. "Oh, really? You didn't have to do that."

Eli shrugged, stuffing his hands into the pockets of the fleece pullover Turner had loaned him. He really should have bought a new coat while shopping, but he hadn't thought about it. He'd been too busy angsting over buying gifts for people he hadn't seen in years.

"I know you like to have a display set up, and I wanted to do it." Eli shuffled nervously. "But you might not like the greeting card. If you want me to take it down tomorrow, I will."

Coach frowned. "You misspell a word or something?"

Eli chuckled nervously. "No."

"Well?"

"You should probably see it for yourself," Turner said. "I think it's quite clever, but ... well, it's not exactly traditional."

Curiosity piqued, Coach got out of his chair. Using his walker, he shuffled out the door. Eli noticed Turner stuck close to his dad, probably in case he slipped, as he slowly made his way down the porch steps and into the yard.

Coach stared at the greeting card, eyes narrowed. Eli cleared his throat. "It'll be easier to read when the lights are on."

"I can read it just fine," Coach said, his voice tight.

"I realize it's a bit much," Eli said cautiously.

"Oh, you do?" His father turned to glare at him. "Then why'd you do it, Eli? Huh? You always pull this shit. You could have gone through high school in peace. You could have left Juniper on good terms. Instead you had to go tell everyone you were gay. And now you're fucking broadcasting it to the entire fucking town!" Coach said, throwing his arms up. He lost his balance, nearly falling, and Turner grabbed his arm to steady him.

Coach shook him off, snapping, "I'm fine."

"I didn't plan it, okay?" Eli said, his stomach twisting with knots. He knew Coach wouldn't like it, but it still hurt to hear his dad confirm everything he'd always thought. He didn't want people to know Eli was gay. It was one thing to accept that he couldn't change it, but part of Coach wanted it to be hidden. Like it was something shameful. "The guy at the hardware store was a jerk. He made some crack about having a homo in town for the holidays, and I got pissed off."

"And this is your answer?" Coach asked, gesturing to the display. "Make sure everyone knows there's a homo in town?"

"Coach," Turner said, a warning in his voice, "I know you're pissed, but watch your mouth."

"What did you say to me?" Coach demanded.

"You heard me," Turner said in a low voice. "Your son is gay. I'm bi. Choose your words more carefully."

Coach's mouth pressed in a tight line, and Eli suddenly wanted nothing more than to get out of there before things escalated. Turner had to work with Coach, and he really didn't want his impulsive actions to cause problems.

"Let's just go running," Eli said. "I can take it down tomorrow. I'm sorry. I guess that old bigot pissed me off, and yeah, I did want to shout it to the town. It's my version of 'I'm here, I'm queer, so deal with it.' I know you probably don't understand why I do that. Why I won't just quietly fly under the radar. But that'll never be who I am."

With that, Eli called for Scout and went to hide in Turner's Jeep. He watched through the window, like a coward, as Turner exchanged a few more words with Coach, then stayed and watched as Eli's father made his way back inside.

When Turner finally climbed into the Jeep, he gave a pained smile. "Well, that went well!"

"Sorry," Eli said. "I just had to go there."

Turner patted his knee. "No worries. Let's go run." He winked. "It's great for stress relief."

12

Eli had no doubt that Turner would leave him in the dust, but he hadn't foreseen how his natural clumsiness would come into play. After stretching, during which he'd endlessly amused Turner with his awkward positions, they'd headed down the trail with Scout pacing to Turner's right and Eli on his left.

A handful of steps later, he drifted left while watching Turner's smooth play of muscle at work — if he'd know what a treat it was to watch Turner run, he might have come along before — and inadvertently veered off the edge of the path. His foot caught on a tree limb he didn't see because he was too busy gawking at Turner's pumping thighs, and he tripped.

Eli threw out his hands to break his fall as his ankle turned, and he came down hard. His hands hit the ground, skidding over pebbles, pine needles and twigs that stripped his flesh before he came to a stop in a twisted heap, cursing loudly.

Turner was at his side immediately. "Are you okay?"

Scout ran up, sticking his snout into Eli's neck and making him flinch at the cold, wet nose on him.

"Okay, boy," he said, pushing Scout's head back, only to be licked in the face for his troubles. "I'm okay."

"Scout, calm down," Turner said, dragging the dog back and scooting in closer to Eli. "Are you really okay?"

"Twisted my ankle. Definitely bruised my pride."

A jogger approached from the other direction, her strides even and her ponytail bouncing behind her. She slowed as she approached them, looking like one of those slow-motion scenes from freaking *Baywatch* but with less jiggle. Her sports bra kept her girls in check, but she had ample cleavage on display and legs for days.

Turner's eyes brightened. "It's Desiree. This is your lucky day."

Eli wasn't sure how pissing off his father and then humiliating himself in front of Turner was lucky — and he was *gay*, so the bombshell on the path didn't do much for him either.

"Hey, Des, did you still have that first aid kit in your car?" Turner called as she slowed to a stop.

So he knew Desiree well enough to shorten her name and to be aware of the contents of her car. Great.

Scout abandoned his mission to lick Eli to death and ran to Desiree, bumping his head into her leg. She grinned and scratched behind his ears. *So Scout likes her too,* Eli thought sourly. *Fantastic.*

"I'm a Girl Scout," she said, "prepared for anything." She looked down at the dog and proceeded to talk in a higher voice. "Isn't that right, Scout? We're always prepared, aren't we? Aren't we?"

Turner snorted, and Eli might be hallucinating, but he could swear there was a sexual tone to that snort.

"I remember," Turner said.

That was definitely sexual innuendo, damn it.

Eli tried to stand up, hissing in pain and drawing Turner's attention back to him. Better. He hadn't intended to make a total fool of himself, but if he was going to be so good at it, he could at least milk it for attention.

"Meet me at the car," Desiree said, and took off at a brisk jog.

Turner had unhooked his leash to Scout at some point, and he pointed after Desiree. "Go with Des, boy. Go help her!"

Scout took off, yipping happily as he ran.

"Didn't want him getting in the middle," Turner said. "Let me help you up."

He pulled Eli's left arm over his shoulder and took some of his weight as Eli hopped on his right foot. His left foot felt like a heavy weight hanging on the end of his leg. Not good.

"Damn, did it hurt this much when you jumped from that swing and landed wrong? Because this fucking hurts."

Turner chuckled. "Oh yeah. But the adoration of my fourth-grade fans made it worthwhile. You were especially impressed, if I remember right."

"I can't help noticing you don't look particularly impressed right now," Eli grumbled.

"I'm impressed at your level of klutziness, Eli. I'm downright awed."

"Funny."

Eli burned up with embarrassment despite the chill in the air as Turner helped him hobble to the parking lot. He hadn't exactly been smooth since reconnecting with Turner. So far, he'd cut off his student driver, gotten stuck in the snow, nailed the man with a dart, and now proven he couldn't run a few feet without injuring himself.

Meanwhile, Turner seemed a little too interested in Desiree's ass as she bent in the open door of her car and retrieved the first aid kit. Unable to help himself, he jabbed Turner in the ribs.

Turner grunted. "What?"

"You're staring at her ass."

"No," he said calmly, "I was just watching while she grabbed the kit. Come on, let's get you into the Jeep."

Turner opened the back passenger door of his Jeep and helped Eli onto the seat. Considering he had only one foot and the seat was high, that involved an embarrassing game of hop off one foot while Turner grabbed his waist and hoisted him up like a damn kid.

For a breathless moment, Turner leaned intimately close, his hands still on Eli's hips. "You're heavier than you look."

"I'm not actually a child, despite our height difference."

Turner grinned, making Eli's heart flutter. "I'm well aware."

"How do you know her?" Eli asked.

Turner glanced over his shoulder, then winced a little. "She's my ex."

"Another ex," Eli said. "How many of those do you have wandering around? Should I expect one every time we're out together?"

Turner lifted his eyebrow at Eli's snarky tone, and he realized he should dial it down a notch. "Sorry, I get bitchy when I'm in pain."

"I've only dated two people since I've been back from college," Turner said evenly. "Cam and I were fairly serious, but we weren't compatible enough to make it work. Desiree and I were more casual. We've been kind of on again, off again. More friends with benefits, I guess you'd say."

"She looks like she'd like to offer you some more benefits right now," Eli grumbled.

"Be nice. She's helping you out."

She wasn't there for Eli's sake, but he clamped his mouth shut as she approached. "Here you go," she said, giving Eli a once-over. "Have we met?"

"Don't think so. I'm Eli," he said, holding out a bloodied hand, then pulling it back. "Sorry. Probably don't want to shake that."

She smiled. "Eli...?"

"Harp," Eli said at the same time Turner said, "An old friend."

Well, thanks Turner. Now Eli felt like about as special as an old sock. But Desiree's eyes widened. "Oh, *Eli*. I've heard about you. You're Coach's son."

Eli nodded. Desiree didn't elaborate, leaving him in the dark as to whether she'd heard about him from Turner specifically or just because he was Coach's son. He was willing to bet it was the latter.

Turner took the first aid kit from Desiree. "Thanks, darlin'. "

Darlin', really? Desiree smirked and swatted his butt. "You know I've got your backside."

Gag. Eli felt bile climb his throat. Leave it to Desiree to be flattered rather than insulted by an empty endearment. Then again, looking at them smile at each other, Eli wondered if maybe it wasn't so empty. Turner said they were on and off. Were they currently on? Surely Turner wouldn't have kissed Eli if that were the case. But then he had called it friendly, and Eli would be leaving after the new year, so maybe Turner didn't think it worth mentioning. Not like they were committed to each other, was it? Even if Eli's heart did excited cartwheels whenever he saw Turner. Even if it melted for him like it had for no one else ever.

Desiree stepped back as Turner gently pulled off Eli's shoe, making him whimper like a goddamn baby. "Shh. I'm trying to be gentle," Turner said, glancing up.

Eli looked into his dark eyes and couldn't breathe for how much he wanted him. How could he have gone years without feeling this yearning, but a few days back home and he was hopelessly pining again? The expression that distance makes the heart grow fonder was clearly a lie. Proximity, that was what made his pulse race. He needed to get the heck out Juniper if Turner really wanted nothing more than friendship.

Eli just had to get through Christmas and New Year's, then find a new job — and a new apartment since things with his roommate were going south. Basically figure out his entire life going forward. No biggie.

"Eli, you with me?" Turner asked as he carefully prodded Eli's ankle.

Eli bit down on his lip until he tasted blood, but that was better than whimpering again at the pain.

"It's swelling a bit," Turner said. "Doesn't look too awful."

"Don't forget to RICE," Desiree said.

Eli nodded, familiar with the term thanks to growing up surrounded by athletes. RICE was an acronym for treating sprains. It stood for rest, ice, compression, and elevate. Eli would have to stay off his feet, ice his ankle, wrap it up, and then elevate it on pillows to keep the swelling down. With any luck, he wouldn't end up in the ER getting X-rays. His health insurance through his employer lasted until the end of the month, thankfully, but he'd rather not pay his share of the bill while unemployed. He'd already spent enough on gas to make the trip here and Christmas gifts for his and Turner's families.

Turner lifted Eli's hands and blew over his shredded palms embedded with pine needles and dirt. "This needs to be disinfected."

What followed was more embarrassment. Eli couldn't keep back the hiss of discomfort as Turner tortured him with alcohol and peroxide wipes and picked debris from his skin. Once finished, Turner bandaged Eli's palms.

"There. Now, what about your knees?"

He pushed up one pant leg, fingers brushing along Eli's calf and sending tingles over his skin.

Eli promptly choked on his own saliva.

"Is he okay?" Desiree asked.

"Choked on my spit," Eli wheezed as Turner laughed, patting him on the back.

"You're a mess. I'll take you home." Turner repacked the first aid supplies and handed the box back to Desiree. "Thanks."

"Anything for you, babe. Are we on for coffee next week?"

"Wouldn't miss it."

Eli glared as hard as he could from behind Turner's half-turned body. Desiree met his eyes once and smirked. Then she leaned in and whispered something in Turner's ear before kissing his cheek and finally withdrawing.

Turner looked like the cat who'd caught the canary when he turned back to Eli.

"Let's get you home so you can ice up. Your poor mother is going to have two lame men tonight."

Turner helped Eli into the house while Scout danced around them, a mix of excited and concerned. Thankfully, his dog seemed to realize something wasn't quite right with Eli and kept enough distance that he didn't trip them.

"I feel like such an idiot," Eli said through clenched teeth as he clung to Turner. "God, you must love me hanging all over you."

Turner did, actually. Eli was pressed up along Turner's side, an arm wrapped around his shoulder, so close that Turner could smell their combined sweat. He felt a niggle of guilt for enjoying it when Eli was in pain and clearly embarrassed.

"It's fine, Eli. People fall," Turner said. "Don't beat yourself up over it."

He got Eli through the door and halfway to the couch before he remembered they'd left a disgruntled Coach behind earlier.

"What happened?" he asked as Turner lowered Eli onto the sofa and gently propped his puffy ankle on the coffee table.

"Eli twisted his ankle when we tried to run."

Coach snorted. "Should have seen that coming."

"Well, thanks," Eli said sarcastically. "I guess I won't bother *trying* again."

Turner grabbed a throw pillow for good measure, propping Eli's foot up a little higher.

"Didn't mean it like that. Just that we'd barely gotten started." He winced. That didn't sound much better, and Eli didn't look any happier with his word choice. "Let me get you some ice before I go."

Coach said almost offhandedly, "Guess you won't be able to take down that holiday display."

Turner glanced up at Eli in time to catch his expression of dismay. "Shit, I'm sorr—"

"We'll just have to leave it," Coach said calmly.

"I might have just twisted the ankle. If it's better tomorrow ..."

"Just leave it, Eli," Coach replied. "If nothing else, it'll tell assholes like Mike Kraft that I'm on your side."

Turner heard Eli's breath catch. "You are?"

Coach looked over. "Of course I am. You're my kid," he said. "I don't understand you, Eli, or your need to throw it all out there. But I'm not ashamed of you, and I don't want you to feel ashamed of yourself either."

Eli swallowed hard. "Thanks, Dad."

It was the first time Turner had heard Eli call the man Dad since he'd returned. Smiling to himself, Turner went to the kitchen to hunt up an ice pack.

Molly was in the living room, examining Eli's ankle, when Turner returned. She took the ice pack from him. "I'll see to it," she said. "Have a seat."

"Oh, I should go. Scout's going to be a pest."

She glanced over at Scout, curled up near the Christmas tree, despite not getting his full run in. H looked to be as well behaved as he ever was. "Yeah, he looks like a real trouble-maker."

Turner laughed and relented, easing down on the sofa near Eli as Molly carefully wrapped the ice pack around his ankle. "How's it feel?"

"Cold," Eli grumped.

"We were just getting ready to settle in with a holiday movie. You two should join us," Molly said.

"Well, I had plans to go dancing tonight," Eli quipped, "but I suppose ..."

Turner chuckled. "You didn't really, did you?"

Eli gave him a look that made him flush with embarrassment. Yeah, he'd obviously been kidding. There were no gay clubs in Juniper, and the ones for straight couples were a little too country for Eli's tastes.

Turner wasn't ordinarily this uncertain of himself, but he didn't know where he stood with Eli. Despite Desiree whispering that Eli looked positively smitten with him, he wasn't sure what Eli wanted, and Turner was having a hard time keeping to friendly terms as planned. Resisting Eli when they were teens had cost him so much. This felt like his chance to have everything he'd been missing, even if only for a while.

But did Eli feel the same?

"Turner?" Eli prompted, waving a bandaged hand in front of his face. "You in there?"

"Hmm? Sorry. I was spacing out."

Eli smirked. "Mom wants to know if you're going to stay and watch a movie with us?"

"Oh, I shouldn't. I've got school in the morning—"

"It's only six," Molly said. "I've ordered a pizza, and we've got plenty of popcorn. Relax a little, Turner."

He glanced down at his running attire. Not the coziest for watching movies, but then he caught another glimpse of Eli's pleading eyes. "Just for a while, then ..."

Turner felt fingers slip along his back, between his shirt and pants, and flinched before realizing it was Eli's hand. Slowly, a finger stroked over his skin. "I vote for 'A Christmas Story.' " Eli said casually, a mischievous look in his eye. "What do you say, Turner?"

"Sounds good to me," Turner said, blanking on what movie it was and not even caring as Eli continued to trace patterns over his skin. "Whatever you want."

"Finally, a year I can escape without watching 'A Wonderful Life,' " Coach said with relief.

Molly laughed good-naturedly. "Looks like I'm outvoted."

Turner glanced her way. "Oh, I shouldn't get a vote. Don't listen to me."

She smiled. "No, it's fine. I'm just happy to have all my family here." She smiled at the both of them on the couch. "It's good to see you boys together again."

Yes, but for how long?

13

December 17th

Turner wasn't surprised to see Desiree turn up at his office during Monday's lunch hour. She worked as the physical education teacher at Juniper High. They'd been hooking up casually when it suited them, but neither of them felt that special spark. It was more about meeting a need in a small town with limited options.

"Hey, Mr. T," she said lightly. "Can I come in?"

He closed his laptop and looked at her over his desk. "Sure."

"I'm not interrupting any plans for a quickie?" she checked.

He scowled. "You know you're not."

Despite hooking up with a teacher, Turner had never fooled around on school property. That was asking for trouble. She knew that he wouldn't do that, so this was just her way of fishing for details.

Des plopped into a seat and kicked her long legs up onto his desk. She wore yoga pants that hugged her slim limbs and a sports tank top. Turner lifted his eyes to her face before he could appreciate what the form-fitting clothes did for her. Desiree was gorgeous, fun, and easygoing. They'd fallen into bed not long after meeting, and they had a ton in common. Aside from running, they both liked dogs and the same kind of movies. But despite all that, there was just some essential ingredient missing between them. Turner had never felt anything more than fondness for her.

"Just say it," he said.

"You and Eli Harp," she said. "You never told me that story."

"I did, actually," Turner said. "I just never told you he was Coach's son."

She crossed her arms over her chest. "So, this is the first guy? The one who got away because you didn't have the guts to be open about being bi?"

Turner glanced behind her toward the halls, but no one was around. His office was far removed from the favorite lunch spots in the school. "That's him."

She suddenly laughed. "Holy crap, you're hot for your boss's son."

Turner shushed her out of habit. "We grew up together. Best friends."

"Aw. You're such a cute cliché," she said. "Falling for your best friend."

Turner scowled. "Glad you're amused, but the fact is this is the first time I've seen Eli in damn near a decade. And I don't know how long he'll be around before he's gone again. So, it's not really all that fun to be a cute cliché."

Her teasing smile slipped. "I'm sorry, Turner. I didn't' realize…"

"He's here for the holidays. He'll go back to California soon enough."

"What are you going to do?" she asked.

Turner thought back to the night before, when Eli had teased his fingers along Turner's back and just under the waistband of his pants until Turner had to fake being cold and grab a throw blanket to hide his hard-on. Which had just encouraged Eli to slip his hand onto his thigh. When he'd edged toward Turner's dick, Turner had grabbed his hand and held it the rest of the movie.

With an excuse to hold his hand — and finally end the torment — Turner had sat back and relaxed, laughing as Ralphie begged for his BB gun and ran afoul of his cranky father. He'd enjoyed holding Eli's hand and just being close to him, and the way Molly had looked at them, Turner was pretty sure she knew they were feeling more than friendship.

But that didn't change the reality. Eli didn't live in Juniper, and Turner — despite being single —was tied down by family obligations.

"I don't know," he said. "Make the most of the time we have, if he lets me."

"He'd be a fool not to," Desiree said, standing now that she'd gotten the intel she wanted out of him. "Besides, you never know how life will work out. Maybe he'll go home and be so heart-broken without you he races right back into your arms."

Turner rolled his eyes. "This isn't a Hallmark movie. But thanks for the vote of confidence."

Eli shifted on his bed, his tight jeans riding up uncomfortably. Turner had texted to make sure Eli still felt up to going out and cruising holiday lights — he'd answered that Turner wasn't getting out of their deal, even if he *had* ended up watching a holiday movie the night before — and now he was fidgeting nervously on his bed while talking to Barb, who'd called just in time for Eli to vomit up all his angst.

Turner had held his hand during the movie, but only as a means to stop Eli's teasing. He didn't know what it meant, if anything. Eli had made up his mind from the moment Turner kissed him that he wanted Turner and not in a friendly way. He didn't care that he wasn't staying in Juniper. Waste not, want not. That was the expression

But he was oddly bothered by Desiree. She was beautiful and bosomy, the perfect match for Turner. The one he'd probably go to the minute Eli was gone, if not before then. It was silly to be jealous when he wasn't even going to be staying in Juniper after the new year, but there it was. He was jealous.

"You should see her boobs, Barb. No way I can compete with that," he said.

"Do you want to compete with her?" Barb asked, cutting to the heart of the matter. This is why she got the big bucks, and Eli got the chopping block.

"I'm not staying in Juniper." he said. "I can't have a future with Turner. But, yeah, I want to be with him while I'm here at least."

"You're not on a time schedule, you know."

"Sure, I am. The holidays won't last forever."

"You don't have a job," she reminded him. "You could stay in Juniper until you're sure of what you want."

That made his palms sweat. "I spent my entire high school career just dreaming of getting out. My teenage self would kick my ass if I moved back after all I went through."

"Priorities change," she said simply. "I'm just saying you have time to figure out what's best for your future. And what you want with your friend."

"Maybe." He groaned. "I haven't even taken a look at my resume yet."

"I'm so sorry I couldn't save your job."

"Not your fault," Eli said. "It's good I came here."

"How's it going with your family then?" she asked, sounding truly interested.

Eli filled her in on the latest, including the shocking revelation that after being initially furious Coach had let his gay pride holiday greeting stand in his front yard, apparently willing to leave it through the rest of the season. They chatted about the merger

she was undergoing, his apartment troubles with his roommate —
"I knew he'd end up being a problem," she said unhelpfully — and
where he should start with the job hunt after the holidays.

He was so busy chatting he didn't notice the time until a tap
at the door drew his attention to the man in question. Turner
stood in his doorway, looking gorgeous in a maroon sweater and
jeans. Forget all his mom's holiday desserts, Eli decided this was
the most mouth-watering treat he'd seen yet.

"Sorry, Barb, I've got to go," Eli said. "Turner is here."

"Okay, have fun," she said. "Try not to worry so much about
the future. Everything will work itself out."

Oh, sure. Like it'd worked out so well before. But Barb was
trying to be supportive, so Eli didn't say that. He just said
goodbye and smiled up at Turner.

"Sorry, I'm ready. You look nice."

Turner's gazed panned over him. He'd pulled on tight jeans
and a long-sleeved T-shirt, the closest he got to winter wear these
days. "You too," he said. "How's the ankle?"

"A lot better. The swelling went down."

Turner nodded. "That's great." He extended a hand. "Let me
help you out to the car anyway. You should probably go easy on it
for a while."

Use Turner's strong body as a crutch? Such a sacrifice.

Turner and Eli were halfway down the driveway when Eli pulled
up short. "I should drive. You've already carted me around enough
times."

Turner shook his head. "I don't mind. I'd rather drive."

Eli huffed. "Well, maybe I mind. I'm not helpless."

"Come on, Eli. Your ankle is still recovering, and it's best
not to drive while impaired even slightly. I'm a driver's ed
teacher. I know these things." Eli opened his mouth, and Turner

pressed a finger over his full lips. "Just give it up. You don't have much of a leg to stand on." He winked. "And I do mean that literally."

Eli nipped the tip of his finger, and Turner yanked it back.

"You're not as funny as you think you are," Eli said. "But fine, since it means so much to your ego, you drive."

Eli turned, walking down the driveway without Turner's assistance. His ankle really was much better. Turner could detect only a slight limp as Eli made his way to the Jeep. Turner's instinct was to rush forward and open the door for him, but judging by the conversation they'd just had, he settled for watching Eli settle his fine ass into the car seat on his own.

"Where should we start?" Eli asked once Turner had started up the car and shifted into drive. "Is Seacrest Lane still going all out?"

"Not so much anymore. I'll hit Hemingway first, and then I have a few other spots in mind. Unless you have any special requests?"

Eli shook his head. "Sounds good."

While he drove, Eli watched the scenery through the passenger-door window. While junipers and aspens were most common in town, the city had planted pine and fir trees, as well as some maple and cottonwood trees in some of the parks. While the snow had melted on the streets, most of the trees still glistened with a bit of frost.

"I'd forgotten how beautiful it is here," Eli said. "It always smells so fresh, too, with the pine needles. It's not like that in California. Or, it probably is in certain spots, but not my town."

"Do you miss the dog food scent of the brewery too?" Turner asked.

On summer nights, especially, the smell from the brewery on the far end of town carried on the wind. For some strange reason, it smelled like dog food.

Eli snickered. "Some of my fondest teenage memories were

cruising with you with the windows down. Smelling that godawful smell."

"Sucking on a fire stick," Turner added.

Eli had been addicted to the Jolly Rancher candy Turner never saw in the stores anymore. It'd been a form of torture, sitting in his car pretending to be straight while Eli ran his tongue up and down the fire stick to get it wet, then slowly slid it into his mouth. Remembering the slurping sound it made as Eli pulled it free, his lips stained red, made Turner shift in his seat.

Eli grinned at him. "You hated when I bought those."

Hated them for the way he felt watching Eli. At the same time, he couldn't resist watching and thinking about what it'd be like to have that mouth on him.

"I wonder if they sell them at the gas station? I never see them in California anymore."

Turner cleared his throat. "I don't think so."

Thank fuck. There was no way he could watch Eli suck on a fire stick without whipping out his own dick and offering it up as a treat. Then again, he'd be lying to himself if he didn't admit he'd probably end up doing that anyway. Any thoughts of keeping Eli in the friend zone had been incinerated by the hot kiss Eli had laid on him. He could put up a token resistance, but why bother? He wanted Eli.

Turner slowed the Jeep to a crawl as they passed through a brightly lit neighborhood. On this part of Hemingway, the residents worked together, and strings of lights connected one house to the next, with not a single dark house in between. Colored lights wrapped around trees and bushes. Reindeer and snowmen made of wire frames wrapped in white Christmas lights decorated the yards. Some of the lights blinked on and off, and others shone steady. All in all, it was a pretty display — if a rather predictable one.

"Looks the same as it did before I left," Eli murmured, his mind obviously moving along the same track.

"Yeah, this area is pretty traditional," Turner said. "You have to admire their consistency. People have moved out and others in. Still, they keep the display year after year."

Eli glanced at him, a faint smile on his face. "It's nice to know that not everything changes, even when you're gone." He hesitated. "Sometimes, I wondered if anyone at all even thought of me after I left."

Turner locked eyes with him. "I know I did."

Eli could see that Turner meant it. He'd thought of Eli in the years they'd been apart. Maybe as only a friend he missed, but that was something. That was a lot.

"I know your parents thought of you often," Turner added as he turned his attention to the road, accelerating as they left the neighborhood. "There are some cool new displays that have gone up since you left, though. I want to show you one."

"Okay," Eli said hesitantly, feeling as if the moment had passed and he'd somehow missed his chance to grab onto Turner and share a moment. "Thanks for doing this with me."

"A deal's a deal." He glanced over at Eli. "I like hanging out with you, no matter what we end up doing."

Eli knew what he'd really like to do: strip Turner Williams naked and finally kiss and lick that perfect body. But looking at Christmas lights was nice too, so he smiled. "Yeah, me too."

Turner slowed the Jeep to a stop, parking at the curb. Gesturing across the street, he said, "This is the place. They do a light show."

He reached forward, tuning the radio to a new station. Christmas music began to play from the car speakers. Some new spin-off song about jingle bells. As Eli watched, he saw that the lights were in sync with the music. "Oh, cool. They never had anything like this when we were kids."

"I bet they have some cool stuff back in California, though."

"They do, but ... it's a completely different feel. It's always so sunny and warm. It was hard for me to ever really feel the holiday. Not like I do here."

"Makes sense," Turner said. "No place is like home."

"I guess not. I was so focused on the bad memories, I forgot that there were good ones too." He met Turner's dark eyes and smiled wistfully. "Most of the good ones have you in them."

"I wish I could have made them all good for you."

Eli only nodded before cutting his eyes back to the house. He didn't want to dwell on the past, so he watched the holiday display — this one had lights bouncing from trees to deer to snowflakes on the roof. Different colors, different speeds. It was almost hypnotic. Eli thought he could probably sit there for hours watching the lights bounce around in time to the music.

"Eli..."

Eli glanced back at Turner. "Yes?"

"When are you going back to California?"

Eli shrugged. Licking his lips nervously, he admitted, "I'm not sure yet."

"You don't have to get back for work?"

Eli frowned. "Don't tell my parents, but I got laid off right before I came home."

"They canned you right before Christmas?"

Eli chuckled. "Yeah. It sounds bad, but it wasn't my boss's choice. Our shelter merged with another, and suddenly there was no position for me anymore. She was the one who encouraged me to use the time to go home. Actually, she's the one I was talking to when you showed up tonight."

"Barb?" Turner asked.

Eli nodded. "She was my boss, but also a friend. She really cares about those kids. Her own son committed suicide after her husband kicked him out. She was devastated."

"Jesus," Turner said, sounding disturbed. Not exactly a great prelude to sexy times, Eli realized. "Did she agree to let her husband disown her son?"

Eli shook his head. "It happened while she was visiting her sister. She came home to find her son gone and her husband stubbornly refusing to tell her where he'd gone. Next thing she knew, the police were knocking on her door with the news he was dead."

"That's awful."

"Yeah," Eli said softly. "So, she got divorced, and ever since, she's worked to help LGBT kids. To make sure something like that didn't happen to them."

"Did you ever ..." Turner stopped, rubbing a hand over his face. "You didn't, did you?"

Eli understood the unspoken question. "No," he said quietly. "I was pretty low, but I was too angry, I guess. I thought if I just left Juniper, I'd find happiness and true love and prove to everyone that being gay was a good thing. That they were wrong about me."

Turner reached out, taking hold of his hand. "Being gay *is* a good thing. They were wrong about you."

Eli tried to smile. "Thanks. But it hasn't all been a fairy tale. Turns out the world, even outside Juniper, isn't all sparkles and unicorns."

Turner feigned surprise. "You're kidding!"

"Nope," Eli said with a chuckle. "No Prince Charming for this princess."

Turner's hand tightened on his. He took a breath and let it out. "No special guy back home?"

"Not even close," Eli said.

There was a long pause. Long enough that Eli thought the conversation was over. He had just opened his mouth to suggest they move on to the next neighborhood when Turner said, "I've been dying to kiss you again."

Eli swallowed hard. "Yeah, same."

Leaning in slowly, Turner made his intention to kiss Eli clear. Eli was all for it, holding his breath in anticipation as Turner got closer and closer, until their lips brushed. Once again, Turner kept the kiss light, but this time lingered over it, brushing their lips together once, twice, three times, before kissing down Eli's jaw to his neck. Nuzzling him there, Turner said, "I have to go check on Scout. Do you want to come with me?"

Eli felt his heart quicken. "Go to your place?"

"Yep."

"Just to check on Scout, or ..."

Turner sat back, his dark eyes holding Eli's gaze. "Or you could stay for a while."

Eli was down. Lord, was he down. He was ready to *go* down. But he wondered what had changed Turner's mind.

"You said before that we should just stay friends since I'm leaving," Eli said.

"That was before you kissed me stupid," Turner said. "I can't be around you and not want more of that."

Eli chuckled sheepishly. "Sorry. I figured if I was only getting one kiss, I should make it one to remember."

"I've remembered it every night," Turner said, giving him a meaningful look before shifting the car into drive and pulling away from the curb.

"God, me too," Eli admitted, feeling the thick wave of lust move through him now that he knew he wouldn't have to hold back all night.

Turner flashed him a grin. "Sounds like we both want the same thing."

Pressing hot naked flesh with Turner Williams? Yes, please. Eli chose not to think about anything more. Just the urgency of his cock rapidly hardening in his jeans.

"Can't you drive any faster?" Eli asked.

Turner laughed. "I'm a driving instructor," he reminded Eli. But Eli noticed that as soon as they were out of the residential area and onto a commercial street, Turner pressed the gas pedal a little harder. Five minutes later, he was turning into his driveway and killing the engine.

Eli unbuckled his seat belt and flung himself at Turner, kissing him hard. This time, Turner didn't try to keep the kiss chaste, but devoured Eli right back. Thrusting his fingers into Eli's hair, he used his lips and tongue to make love to Eli's mouth until Eli was whimpering, desperate for more.

"Inside?" Turner asked between kisses.

Eli groaned under the onslaught, grasping at Turner's coat. "God, yes, please."

"Unless you want to fuck in the car? After that story about riding surfers ..."

"Shut up," Eli said, tearing himself from Turner's body and grabbing for the door handle. "I made that up to rile you up." He eyed Turner's flushed cheeks and puffy lips. "Looks like it worked too."

"You're gonna pay for that," Turner growled, opening his car door. Then in direct opposition to his tough-guy routine, he said, "Wait there, and I'll help you to my door. I don't want you hurting that ankle."

"Such a gentleman," Eli teased.

Turner helped him out of the car, whispering in his ear. "But not for long, Eli. Soon, you're gonna see how ungentlemanly I can be."

Eli shivered at the words. He couldn't wait to find out.

14

Turner half carried Eli through his front door, nearly tripping over an antsy Scout in the process. "Scout, back!" he ordered as Eli laughed against his neck. Turner had his hands on Eli's ass and no desire to move them anytime soon, so he kicked the front door shut.

Scout paced around them, panting and whining. Turner kissed Eli again, squeezing his ass, until Scout jostled them, whining again.

"Damn it," he muttered against Eli's lips. "Just give me a minute."

"I'll give you two," Eli said with a wink. "As long as we're talking right now. I'm going to need you for significantly longer once we're in bed."

Turner suppressed a groan and turned to his cock-blocking dog. "Okay, buddy. Let's go check your water bowl."

There was no reason for Scout to be so antsy. Turner had gone on his usual run with him, making sure Scout was thoroughly exercised so he wouldn't have to worry about leaving him tonight while he and Eli went to check out holiday lights. Scout had been spoiled lately, though, with so many visits to the Harps' house. If he wasn't careful, Scout was going to try to leave him for Molly's bacon.

Turner patted his leg as he walked into the kitchen, glancing back at Eli, who was standing in the living room where he'd left him, biting down on his bottom lip as he did when nervous. Finally, Turner would get his chance to devour that lip instead, along with the rest of the gorgeous man.

He grabbed Scout's bowl, filled it with water, then took it into a back room where Scout had some toys. "Be a good boy, huh? Let Daddy get some."

Shaking his head at himself, he patted Scout on the head, closed the door, and returned to Eli.

"Sorry for the delay," he said as he drew Eli back into his arms.

"Yeah? You can show me how sincerely sorry you are," Eli teased before licking a stripe up Turner's neck. Turner was rock hard in his jeans, and he ground against Eli, groaning when Eli bit down on his earlobe.

"Fuck," he gasped.

"Not much of an apology," Eli mused.

Turner dropped a hand, massaging Eli's equally hard shaft through the denim of his jeans. "How's this?"

"Better," Eli murmured, pushing into his hand. Turner popped his jeans button, then pulled down his zipper.

"How about we continue this horizontally?" Eli asked, shifting on his feet as Turner leaned into him.

"Right, the ankle. Sorry." Turner scooped Eli up and slung him over his shoulder.

Eli cried out in surprise. "Turner!"

Turner carried Eli into his bedroom and laid him out in the center of the bed. As fun as it might be to drop him and watch him bounce, he didn't want to aggravate his injury.

"You look just as good there as I thought you would."

Eli smiled up at him impishly. "Been picturing me in your bed, Turner?"

"You have no idea," he said hoarsely. Crawling up over him, Turner said, "The fantasy does have one advantage, though."

"What's that?"

"We're both already naked."

Eli's tongue darted out to lick his lips. "That can be arranged," he said.

Turner leaned down to trace his own tongue along Eli's bottom lip. For a minute, he indulged in all the desires he'd suppressed as he'd watched Eli lick and nibble at his lip these past few days. He licked Eli's lip, kissed it, drew it between his teeth and sucked on it.

Eli gasped against him, clutching his arms, while Turner worshipped that teasing mouth. Finally, when dots danced in his eyes, he drew back to breathe. Eli's chest heaved beneath him.

"Holy hell," he said faintly. "Nobody's ever kissed me like that before."

And nobody else ever will. The words roared inside Turner, but he didn't say them, knowing he didn't have a claim on Eli. He settled for smiling smugly. "I'm just getting started."

Eli laughed breathlessly. "Yeah, what's next?"

Turner eyed his lips. "I don't think I'm done with that mouth."

"No?" Eli's breath quickened. "You might have to lose the pants."

Turner grimaced. "See, this is where the fantasy was more convenient," he teased. "Clothes just vanish."

Eli snapped his fingers. "Damn, didn't work. Get your ass off the bed and get naked."

Turner chuckled, moving away to tug off his T-shirt and unfasten his jeans. Eli watched him with a palpable hunger as each inch of skin was bared. Turner felt his flesh prickling, much as he had the day Eli saw him in his towel, but tonight, he welcomed it as his nipples and cock tightened in concert. He yanked down his jeans and underwear, dragging them over his feet.

Once naked, he let Eli look his fill, riding the high of Eli's admiration. The guy had never been able to hide his true feelings, and his want for Turner was written all over his face. Not to mention his hard cock, which had to be hurting in those tight jeans.

Turner had unzipped him in the living room, so he hooked his fingers under Eli's waistband and dragged his jeans and underwear down. When the material bunched up around Eli's feet, Turner carefully tugged off his shoes before drawing off the jeans, aware that Eli's ankle wasn't yet 100 percent better. Eli had pulled off his shirt while Turner worked, and Turner took a moment to appreciate the sight before him.

Eli was tanner than Turner remembered, probably from all that California sunshine. His shoulders were a toasty brown even in December, with freckles splashed across them. His body, long and slim, appeared to be flexible, and his nipples were a dusky red that matched his mouth and his cock. There was something so sexy about Eli — his mouth so lush and soft while his dick was so flushed and hard.

"Get down here," Eli ordered.

Turner lost no time in pressing their bare skin together. Eli felt even better than he looked, and Turner shuddered.

"Want you so much," Eli gasped.

Turner kissed him again, rolling his hips against Eli, their cocks bobbing and sliding in an uncoordinated grind that was more tantalizing than satisfying. Turner pulled back, breathing hard. Looking into Eli's eyes, he murmured, "I've never been with such a beautiful man."

Eli tried to smile. "Just lots of beautiful women."

Turner dipped his head, running his tongue along the shell of Eli's ear. "They don't hold a candle to you," he whispered.

Eli was doing his best to keep perspective as Turner all but smothered him with his sex appeal. He was gorgeous, with all his running-toned muscle, and sexy as hell — a little dirtier than Eli expected, but in a good way — but he kept throwing Eli off-balance with moments of soft affection. He looked at Eli like he was something precious, even when he was saying that he wanted to put his mouth to good use.

But Eli wasn't in bed with a boyfriend. He was in bed with a man he might never have again. And if he did have him again, their time would be limited. That didn't change the fact that Turner was the love of his life, though, and he fell further and further under his spell as he kissed and licked and rubbed all over Eli.

"Let me suck your dick," Eli pleaded, needing something to break the intensity of their eye contact.

Turner sat up, straddling Eli, and shuffled forward on his knees until his cockhead bumped Eli's mouth. Eli parted his lips, darting his tongue out to lick up a pearl of precum. He closed his eyes, savoring it. When he opened them, Turner was backing up.

"Where are you going?" Eli complained.

"What? Did you think you were going to have all the fun?" Turner asked. He continued to shuffle down the bed, then turned around, which put his mouth near Eli's cock, and his cock near Eli's mouth. His intention was obvious, and Eli rolled onto his side and grasped the base of Turner's cock to bring it to his mouth.

Turner fisted Eli's cock at the same time, his hand engulfing Eli's shaft.

"Your hands are so fucking big," Eli said with a groan. His gaze went to the cock in front of his face. "All of you is big."

"That's what I've been telling you," Turner teased. "All those times you commented on my huge heart."

He sucked Eli's cock into his mouth, and Eli cried out, instinctively rolling his hips forward. He remembered after a moment of bliss that he was supposed to be sucking Turner too and clumsily stuffed his cock into his mouth.

Turner groaned around Eli's cock, and Eli moaned in response, sucking Turner harder. They mirrored each other, speeding up and slowing down in sync as they worked each other's cocks. Eli squeezed Turner's heavy balls, and Turner made a garbled sound, then retaliated by pressing a wet finger into the crease of Eli's ass. He traced around Eli's hole, setting him on fire. Eli pulled off Turner's cock long enough to say, "Yes, please, finger me," and then he was sucking Turner's cock deep at the same moment a thick finger pushed into him.

He whimpered, bucking his hips between Turner's sucking mouth and his plunging finger, and came suddenly.

He made a muffled sound, sucking harder on Turner's dick as his climax swept through him, and was rewarded with a deep groan as Turner's cock pulsed on his tongue, spurting cum.

Eli rode out his orgasm, Turner's finger still inside him, being squeezed by his fluttering asshole. He almost wished they hadn't just come because he wanted Turner inside him, filling him up. He ground back against Turner's finger as his last drops were wrung out, then let Turner's softening cock slip from his mouth.

"Wow, that was unbelievable." Turner turned around, collapsing with his head next to Eli, and kissed him gently. "Thank you for sucking my brains out."

"Thank you for finger-fucking my cum out."

Turner snorted. "Oh man, your mouth."

"What about it?"

"Sexy and sassy," Turner murmured.

Eli smiled. "And fuckable?"

"That too. Damn."

They lay beside each other, catching their breath, and Eli waited for a cue about how to proceed. Had this been a one-time thing for Turner? Did he want to fuck regularly until Eli went back to California? Eli would take any offer on the table. He had no pride when it came to this man. He just wanted to be with him, however he could.

Turner rolled over and nuzzled his neck. "Being with you was better than I ever imagined."

Eli's heart squeezed painfully in his chest. Turner was using past tense. Was that it for them then?

"Same here," he managed.

Turner kissed his neck, then his shoulder. "I'm gonna get some water and check on Scout. You want some?"

"Yeah," Eli answered, because regardless of what came next, he'd swallowed Turner's cum and could do with a glass of water. He'd figure out the rest later.

Turner smiled, pecked his lips, then went into the next room naked. A moment later he heard Turner curse.

"What is it?" Eli called, easing off the bed and venturing into the doorway. Turner held up a large box of chocolates. It had been torn open, and the candy inside was gone.

"I think Scout gorged on chocolate," he said, looking grim.

Eli didn't own a dog, but even he knew that was bad. "Oh, no!"

Turner spun on his heel, hurrying into the back of the house. "Scout! You okay, boy?" A moment later, he returned. "Get dressed. I have to get him to the vet."

"How is he?" Eli asked as he searched the floor for his clothes, dragging on fabric as quickly as he could.

"I don't know," Turner muttered. "He vomited all over the back room. I should have realized something was wrong."

"He looked fine," Eli said lamely.

"Damn it," Turner cursed. "I was so stupid, leaving that chocolate there. I should have put it up higher. And then I left him here all evening—"

"Turner, stop guilting yourself," Eli said. "Let's just get him to the vet, okay?"

Turner swallowed hard, nodding. "Yeah, okay. Let's go."

Turner rushed ahead as Eli walked gingerly behind him. His ankle was much better than it was, only a little sore, and he managed with only a tiny limp. When he saw Scout panting and whining, his heart squeezed. He couldn't imagine how Turner felt as he gathered his dog in his arms and stood up.

Eli went ahead to open the door for him, then held the back car door open as well so Turner could gently slide Scout onto the backseat. He looked so distressed that Eli said, "I'll sit next to Scout. Or I can drive, if you want?"

Turner shook his head. "Just sit with him so he's not alone." He cleared his throat. "I need to drive, or I'll lose my shit before we ever get there."

Eli nodded and slid in, then reached forward to squeeze Turner's shoulder from behind when he'd gotten into the driver's seat and buckled up.

"I feel like a jackass," Turner said, "not noticing him when we first got there. If he doesn't make it ..."

"He'll make it," Eli said firmly.

"Shouldn't have left him home alone so long. Thinking with my dick."

Eli winced. He knew he'd strongly encouraged Turner to think with his dick, but a part of him had believed he was more than a fuck, even if they couldn't make any commitments.

Turner was turning onto Main Street, two blocks south of Eli's neighborhood when his phone rang. He jabbed the button on the stereo display that showed the caller ID. Mom.

"Hey, what's up?" Turner asked in a voice that masked his emotions impressively well. He sounded abrupt, maybe, but not upset.

"I can't find my new pills. I got a refill like you suggested, but I can't find them."

"Did you look in the bathroom cabinet?"

"I looked everywhere, Turner! I just keep thinking about Christmas and your Dad, and—" Her voice broke. "I just can't turn it off. It's hard."

"I know, Mom. Can you call Krystal? I'm in the middle of something right now."

"I tried, but she didn't answer. She's probably ignoring my call on purpose!"

Turner's hands tightened noticeably on the wheel, and his eyes met Eli's in the rearview mirror. Scout whimpered, and Eli saw the panic flood Turner's eyes. He couldn't help his mother right now, but she was becoming increasingly distraught as they talked.

"Mom, let me try to reach Krystal myself. I'll call you right back," Turner said, hitting disconnect, then slamming a fist down on the steering wheel. "Fuck!"

Eli put a hand on his shoulder. Turner tried to shrug him off, but Eli squeezed. "Turner, pull over."

"What?"

"Pull over here and let me out."

Turner slowed the car, easing over to the curb. "I'm sorry. You probably don't feel safe—"

"Hush and listen," he said. "I'm gonna get out of the car and walk back to my house. I'll drive to your mom's and make sure she's okay so you don't have to worry about anything while you're with Scout."

"But... your ankle."

"It's only a couple of a blocks. I can handle it." Eli opened the car door and stepped out. "Take care of Scout, Turner. I'll check in later."

"God, I'm sorry. This has got to be the worst hookup of your life."

"You'd be wrong about that," Eli said lightly.

He shut the door and backed up, watching Turner drive away. Turner wasn't saying anything untrue. Eli was a hookup, if only because he wouldn't be sticking around Juniper. It still put a sour taste in his mouth. From the moment they'd kissed, he'd set his sights on getting out of the friend zone and into Turner's bed. Now, he had to face the reality that sex was never the only thing he'd wanted.

But he'd deal with those feelings later.

For now, he had a few blocks to walk on a tender ankle and an upset woman to reassure. He wasn't her son, but he'd grown up spending enough time in her house that he wasn't a stranger either. He hoped he could help her find some peace of mind, so that in turn, he could help Turner do the same after he finished with the vet.

Assuming that Scout recovered.

Please, if ever there was a Christmas miracle, let it be that Scout is okay. That man loves his dog.

15

Turner's mother opened the door with red-rimmed eyes. "Eli," she said, tugging her robe a little tighter around her, "you didn't need to come over. I'm fine."

Eli took in the blush on her cheeks, a sure sign she was embarrassed, and lied. "I was out anyway. I had to get some more about that delicious eggnog. You're on the way to the store, so it's no trouble to stop by."

"Oh. Well, I suppose that's okay then."

Eli stepped inside, warmth stinging his cold cheeks. Mrs. Williams had cranked up the heat, and Eli tugged off his beanie and ran a hand through his hair. He was feeling less than clean, the sweat of sex with Turner still on his skin, but it couldn't be helped.

"You were looking for some medication?" he asked, when Turner's mother continued to hover near the front door.

She waved a hand. "Oh, it's fine. I couldn't sleep is all. I can wait until Turner is free."

Eli didn't want to add to her worries, if that's what was keeping her from sleep. But he also didn't want her to wonder why Turner wouldn't help her. He compromised.

"Mrs. Williams—"

"Call me Daisy."

"Daisy," Eli said, "Turner is busy because Scout isn't feeling well. He's taking him to the vet."

Her hand flew to her chest. "Oh, no. That poor dear."

Eli didn't know if she meant Turner or Scout, but he figured the sentiment worked in either case. He nudged her toward the dining room. The house looked the same as Eli remembered from when he'd stop by as a kid. A simple bungalow — practically a replica of Turner's, but two times larger — the living room led straight into a dining room, with the galley-style kitchen tucked behind a swinging door. On the opposite side of the living room, a short hall led to two bedrooms and a bathroom.

"How about we sit down?" Eli suggested.

Daisy led him to the table, then opened a cookie jar and offered him a cinnamon-dusted sugar cookie. Eli grinned. "I haven't had one of these since I left Juniper. Thank you."

"Take two," she encouraged. "Or three. I could make some tea?"

Eli was anxious to get back to Turner, but it was important that Daisy was calm when he left, so he nodded and smiled. "Thanks, that'd be great."

Once she'd filled the kettle and put it on the stove, she finally opened up about the medication. "Ever since Tom died, I've really struggled around the holidays. All the days, really," she said with a sad laugh, "but especially the holidays."

"That makes sense. It's when you're used to having your loved ones near."

She nodded, blinking hard. "It's not only that. I feel ... adrift? Hal was my anchor. Somewhere along the way, I relied on Hal too much. Forgot how to live on my own." She shrugged. "And now, I'm doing the same thing to Turner. I hate how much I ask of him, but I just don't know how I'd cope without him."

The teapot whistled, and she got up, saving Eli from having to agree with her. Turner seemed to have a lot of responsibility pressed on those broad shoulders. While Daisy poured the tea, Eli searched the table — which contained a fair amount of clutter, from junk mail to old newspapers, to a pile of receipts — but he didn't spot any prescription bags.

He stood, checking the buffet that sat against one wall, then ventured to the kitchen doorway. Two grocery bags sat beside the microwave. Eli peeked inside. A box of Special K, a package of Ritz crackers, and a summer sausage filled one bag. The other held a box of tissues and a prescription bag.

"Do you want milk or honey in your tea?" Daisy asked.

"Milk is good." Eli pulled out the small white bag holding a prescription. Turning, he said, "Is this what you were looking for?"

Daisy looked over. "Yes! Where was it?"

Eli gestured behind him to the grocery bags. Daisy set his cup down on the counter and peeked into the bags. "Oh! I swear I put this away. I'd forget my own head if it weren't attached. Getting old is the pits."

Eli handed her the prescription. "It happens to the best of us."

She smiled. "You're being kind, but I know better. I'm old."

"How about we have that tea?" Eli said. "It would be a shame to waste it."

Turner returned to his house, exhausted but relieved. The vet had induced more vomiting, and they were keeping Scout overnight to administer fluids, but he was expected to make a full recovery. Turner still felt guilty for not realizing something was wrong when he'd given him water and shut him in the spare room. If he hadn't been so caught up in Eli, but ... there was no point placing blame. Eli would be gone soon, and Turner couldn't regret being with him. Even if he had spectacularly blown his attempt at friendship with Eli — quite literally, too. He remembered the weight of Eli's cock in his mouth, the firm flesh of his ass in his hands, and shuddered.

Thinking with your dick again.

But fuck, what was so wrong with that? Turner's dick happened to like Eli. The rest of Turner did too. Too much, probably, but he'd cope with that when Eli left. He wasn't going to waste more time trying to resist the inevitable. But he *would* keep a much closer eye on Scout — and the rest of his responsibilities. He couldn't forget that his family needed him.

Speaking of family, he should call and check up on his mother. He tugged his phone out of his pocket and found a new text from Eli.

Eli: *I found your Mom's meds. She's absolutely fine. How is Scout?*
Turner: *He's staying overnight. They say he should be okay*
Eli: *I'm glad to hear that. I'll tell Daisy*
Turner: *You're still there?*
Eli: *Leaving now. Are you still at the vet?*
Turner: *I'm back home*
Eli: *I'm coming over*

When Eli arrived, Turner opened the door with a tired smile. "You didn't have to come over."

Eli drew him into a soft kiss. "I wanted to be here."

"I'm not much in the mood for anything," Turner admitted. "It's been a fucking long night. I already called in to the school to let them know I wouldn't be in tomorrow. The vet says Scout's going to fine, but I still feel so fucking guilty for not realizing something was wrong sooner."

"You can't blame yourself," Eli said. "I know I was a big distraction, but I Googled chocolate poisoning in dogs while I was with your mom. It says it takes a while for symptoms to show up. And one of the symptoms is hyperactivity. That's Scout all the time."

Turner sighed. "It hardly matters now."

"You're right," Eli said with a nod. "What you need now is to decompress."

"Is that code for sex?"

"No," Eli said indignantly. "It's code for a shower and bed. To sleep. Come on," Eli said, shepherding Turner toward the bathroom before he could reject Eli's offer. Turner might have been thinking with his dick earlier, he might consider Eli a hookup, but first and foremost, they were friends. And Eli took care of his friends.

Eli slipped past Turner and turned on the shower taps, adjusting the water until it was hot and the room began to steam.

"Are you staying?" Turner asked.

Eli was afraid if he asked Turner what he wanted, he'd tell Eli to leave, so he answered with more confidence than he felt. "That's the plan."

"We can't possibly fit in the shower together," Turner said.

Eli eyed the space. "It could be done, if we got creative." Eli imagined they'd fit just fine if he was on his knees, but tonight wasn't about sex. "But for now, we can take turns. Go ahead and get undressed."

"Okay," Turner said, tugging off his T-shirt. When Eli stood, watching him, he paused with his hand on his belt buckle. "You going to watch me?"

Eli hesitated but shook his head. Too much temptation if he stayed. "I'll put fresh sheets on your bed while you shower. Where do you keep them?"

"Hall closet."

Eli nodded. "Nothing like a shower and fresh sheets to help you relax."

He turned to go, and Turner caught his hand, squeezed it. "Thanks, Eli."

Turner washed up quickly, wrapping a towel around his waist. Eli had finished the bed and was texting on his phone when Turner entered.

He looked up and smiled. "Hey, feeling better?"

"Yeah, you don't have to coddle me. Scout's going to be fine."

Eli kissed Turner's cheek on the way out. "I know. Doesn't mean you don't deserve a little TLC."

Turner watched Eli step into the bathroom and close the door. TLC. Tender loving care. Did Eli mean that literally, or was TLC just one of those things you said when you meant something needed attention? Maybe he was old and outdated, like a house for sale. *Just needs a little TLC.* Turner was the same age as Eli, but for some reason, he felt much older. Maybe because instead of going on after college to live in a new place and make friends and hook up in gay clubs, he'd been in Juniper, trying to keep his mother together in the aftermath of his father's death, taking a job for Coach even though he was still so angry with the man, and settling in to a life of responsibility.

He didn't regret any of it. But he did feel older than his years sometimes.

He dropped the towel and slipped between the clean sheets, sighing as his legs slid over silky, smooth satin. Eli had been right about clean sheets. They felt perfect, and he was halfway to sleep when Eli slid into the bed behind him, pressing up against his back and kissing the nape of his neck.

"Get some rest, and then we'll spoil Scout with love tomorrow."

Turner made a soft sound he barely recognized as coming

from himself. It sounded like contentment. He'd never had anyone take care of him. Not since he was a child anyway.

He drifted into a peaceful sleep.

Eli blinked his eyes open, taking in his surroundings. Not his California apartment. Not his parents' house. Turner's bedroom.

He turned his head on the pillow, meeting Turner's gaze. He was lying propped on an elbow, watching Eli with a soft smile on his lips. "Morning, gorgeous."

Eli was fairly sure there was nothing gorgeous about him in the morning. He hoped he didn't have dried drool on his face. "Hey," he croaked. "Sleep okay?"

"Slept great, thanks to you," Turner said. "Thanks for babying me."

"Turner, something tells me you need someone to spoil you a little. You don't always have to be the guy helping everyone else, you know?"

"I'm not arguing," Turner said. "I just haven't met the right person for that."

Eli's heart clenched, and he sat up to mask his reaction. "Well, I better get going, huh? Have you checked in with the vet about Scout?"

"Eli, wait," Turner said, placing a hand on his back. The warmth of it washed through Eli's body. "I didn't mean that you weren't the right person. I think you really could be. But you don't live here."

"I know," Eli said. "I'm just a hookup."

"I wouldn't say that."

Eli hesitated. "But you did say that. You said it was probably my worst hookup ever, so ..." Eli tried for a smile. "Not like I didn't know it was casual, what with me leaving after the new year. It's fine."

Turner scowled. "Eli, I was worried about Scout last night. God knows what I was thinking or saying. But we know each other way too well, have too much history, for this to be meaningless sex. Don't you think?"

Eli bit down on his bottom lip, and Turner reached out, pulling his lip free. "None of that," he said, leaning in to kiss Eli. "You don't have to be nervous with me. Whatever you feel, it's okay."

"It wasn't meaningless," Eli agreed.

Not even close.

Turner grinned, kissing him again and lingering over his lips this time. "Good," he murmured. "Because I don't want a one-time hookup with you. I want whatever you'll give me for as long as you're here."

Turner had a point. Eli didn't want to pretend this was some casual hookup, but he also didn't want to spend the short time he was in Juniper being sad about a future they wouldn't have. He should just enjoy the present.

"Reality blows," Eli said. "I'd rather live in a fantasy."

He turned, letting his eyes skate over Turner's body and licked his lips. "What about you?"

Turner took the bait, shoving Eli into the mattress and covering his body with his big, muscled frame. "I can think of a fantasy or twenty I'd love to act out with you," he murmured, before kissing him.

When they broke apart, Eli asked, "What about Scout?"

"Already talked to the vet. They say he's doing well, and I can pick him up at ten."

"A few hours from now," Eli said, glancing at the clock. "However will we pass the time?"

Turner dipped down, nipping his jaw. "I think we'll figure something out."

16

December 21st

Turner made an *excellent* Santa Claus. As in excellently hilarious. Eli couldn't stop his wide grin when he saw Turner in the big, red suit Coach ordinarily wore to the holiday team party each year. Instead of filling out the belly, Turner had used the belt to cinch the jacket around his trim waist. The result was a tall, broad Santa in *very* good shape.

"Why, Santa," Eli teased, "you are looking most unlike yourself tonight."

Turner raised an eyebrow, as if to say *really?,* and adjusted his hat self-consciously. The holiday party Coach held for his track and cross-country teams each year was just about to kick off at the Harps' house. In the four days since their scare with Scout, the border collie had returned home and even gotten back into his running routine with Turner. Eli had checked in on Scout while Turner worked and spent his nights in Turner's bed — and in between, he'd fit in another shopping trip with Janine to Waits Winter Tree Farm, where he'd talked to a sheepish Cam and bought his mom a new angel figurine, and a trip to the high school to watch Cassie's holiday play.

Eli and Turner were alone in the living room for the moment. So, Eli leaned in close to speak into Turner's ear, "You are the hottest Santa I've ever seen. I think I'd like you to come down my chimney any night of the year."

Turner dropped his hands to Eli's hips, tugging him closer. "I don't see why Coach couldn't wear the suit. I agreed when I thought he might not be up to attending the party."

Eli dropped a kiss under Turner's ear before drawing back to a respectable distance. His parents knew something was going on. Coach had pulled Eli aside to ask, "Something going on with you two?"

Eli had stuttered out, "Uh, kind of," and Coach had nodded. "Thought so."

That had been the extent of their talk, which for his Dad was extremely progressive. But he'd still rather not hit him with PDA just yet.

Right now, though, Eli and Turner were alone while Coach got dressed for the party, which took a decade since he'd had the surgery, and Molly put the finishing touches on the dessert table she'd set up in the dining room.

She'd made a selection of pies — she was famous for her rhubarb pie, but she'd also made pecan pie, lemon meringue, and banana cream pie — as well as banana-nut bread, cranberry-orange bread, and spice cake. This was one occasion the athletes were free to gorge on goodies, but Molly also reluctantly put out a vegetable and fruit platter for the more health-conscious athlete. There were always one or two who took their condition extremely seriously, to the extent of passing up delicious holiday sweets.

"You should take this as a good sign," Eli said. "He's passing the mantle."

"How do you figure?"

"If he wants you to be Santa, he's handing over the reins to the sleigh, Turner." Eli frowned in the direction of the bedroom. "I wonder if this means he's going to retire."

Turner looked startled. "You think?"

Eli shrugged. "Dad's a control freak. You know that. Why else would he let you have all the glory of playing Santa tonight? He loved that shit. It was one of the only times Coach was ever jolly. He's always loved Christmas."

"Damn, you're right," Turner said. Then he looked aghast. "Does this mean I have to play Santa every year?"

Eli smirked. "Well, at least until Coach gives up the ghost and no longer attends the parties, huh? Or talks to anyone else who does." He pretended to consider the matter carefully. "Yeah, I'd say you're pretty much screwed for the next decade at least."

Turner gave him a dirty look. "You're going on the naughty list."

Eli grinned. "My favorite place to be."

The house was full to the brim with teenagers. Eli, who'd been cheerfully teasing him for being a hot Santa, was becoming withdrawn as he watched the kids chatter. When they were young, Turner and Eli had loved the team parties. They'd had their hair ruffled by cool guys who asked them if they'd be a track star one day and girls who cooed over them, telling them they were adorable. But once they hit high school, it was another story. Turner had joined the track and cross-country teams and was included in the parties by default. Eli hadn't ever taken to running. He hung around the periphery of the party, but he was no longer an adorable nine-year-old. Most of the team ignored him. Not necessarily out of malice, but because he wasn't in their circle of friends.

Turner always made time for Eli. They'd load up plates, and Turner would take a few minutes to put in an appearance before disappearing into Eli's bedroom. They'd gorge themselves on snacks, hang out, and Turner would return in time for Coach's Santa act of giving out gifts — which were always running-related things like water bottles, stopwatches, colorful shoelaces, and beanies with the team logo on them.

That had been their routine every year of high school until the last one — when Eli kissed Turner under the mistletoe, their lips barely making contact before Turner jerked back, terrified someone had seen. He'd lashed out at Eli angrily, out of fear more than anything. Fear that Eli had finally seen through his act. Fear that meant everyone else had too. When he ran into Kara Whitmore, he was only looking for a distraction. He was trying to cool down and already thinking about how to smooth things over with Eli so they could pretend the kiss never happened.

Then she flirted with him, pointed to the mistletoe, and the answer was right there. *Kiss the girl. No one will believe you're into guys.*

And it worked too. Everyone thought he was straight. Including Eli.

Turner poured a cup of punch and took it to Eli, realizing that he'd been keeping his distance from everyone since the party got started.

"Here," he said, holding it out like a peace offering.

Eli took the cup and sipped. "Thanks."

"You okay?"

Eli met his eyes, shadows in their depths. He forced a smile. "Yeah, sure. I'm just feeling like the odd man out. Nothing new at one of these parties."

"I guess not. But they were fun when we were just kids. Remember?"

Eli smiled faintly. "Yeah. Puberty ruins everything."

Turner stepped closer. "Not everything," he said, brushing the back of his hand along Eli's. "Growing up has its advantages."

Eli raised his eyebrows at him. "Oh yeah?"

"I'll tell you about it later."

"Why, Coach Williams, I think you're getting a little fresh with me."

Turner smirked. "No one calls me that. It's Mr. T."

Eli snorted a laugh. "You're kidding. I'm going to start calling you that in—"

He cut off as a female student came up to Turner. "Hey, Mr. T. Great party."

"I wish I could take credit," Turner said. "You know Coach's wife did all the baking for it."

She grinned. "Yeah, what are you going to do when Coach retires? You don't have a wife to decorate and prepare all the food."

Turner chuckled. "Yeah, I'll have to figure that out, won't I?"

"Well, maybe you'll meet someone before that happens."

"For the sake of everyone eating the food at my party, let's hope so," Turner said with a wink.

Eli felt a tightness in his chest and told himself not to be silly. Just because that student had brought up a future wife didn't mean that Turner planned to marry a woman.

But he could. It's an option for him — and a much more likely one than Turner marrying you.

Oh God, he didn't want to marry Turner. Did he? Eli was going back to California after the new year. He'd get a new job and a new apartment and he'd start over.

"I need the bathroom," he said, his stomach giving a sick twist.

He thrust the cup of punch into Turner's hand, ignoring his concerned look, and hurried away for a much-needed minute to clear his head. The fact he'd burned with jealousy at the idea of Turner with a woman — probably that busty Desiree, for fuck's sake — was disconcerting. Eli had returned to Juniper for the holidays to see his family and try to make peace, nothing more. Turner was supposed to have moved away, or at least moved on, because Eli never intended to stay in Juniper. It was too small, too conservative, too close-minded.

His stay could easily extend beyond New Year's. He hadn't even begun to sort out his resume or send in applications anywhere. But it couldn't be permanent.

Eli turned on the faucet and splashed cold water on his face. "Get a grip, Eli," he muttered. "Enjoy Turner, but don't kid yourself about where this is going. Friends. We'll be friends when we part. Good friends, even. We'll stay in touch."

Eli forced himself to remember the harassment he'd experienced in school. The homophobic slurs and veiled threats. The way he'd felt dirty and ashamed, even when he knew he shouldn't. The suffocating desperation he'd felt to escape and be free.

You don't want all that again, even for Turner. Do you?

But even as he remembered those awful days, a part of him recognized that things were different now. For him, at least. He didn't know what a gay kid might experience at Juniper High. But he knew that at least one staff member was bisexual now that Turner was there, and he'd never stood for bullying, even as a teenager himself. He'd step in to shut that shit down. And Cam lived in Juniper, even though he was gay. Hell, there was an LGBT Center and a GSA at the high school, he'd heard. That simply didn't exist when Eli had been younger.

Tim Carrow had been a tool when Eli met him at the bar, but he'd been easily managed. Hardly the hate-spewing, macho threat he'd been in high school. The hardware store owner had been a bigot, too, but he was an old, bitter man not worth Eli's time. Janine had been sweet and funny, picking up their friendship right where they'd left off. There was his mother, who he knew missed him. And Coach was trying, it seemed, to accept Eli for who he was.

He wasn't dumb. Juniper was still a conservative place with plenty of bigots to go around, but he no longer had to subject himself to the mass populace as he did in high school. He could choose who to admit into his circle of friends and family.

"You're not really considering this," he whispered to his reflection. His green eyes blinked at him. "Fuck, you're mental."

He shook his head one last time, pointed at the mirror, and said, "No."

Then he dried his face and returned to the party.

Chris Woods approached at a lope, all long legs and big, white teeth. The kid had shot up three inches over the summer, and he was already their fastest sprinter, though Rachelle Liesen on the girls team was still their most talented distance runner. Troy Matthews was a close second. They ran different events — since women and men were separated — but Rachelle was smashing records every time she ran.

"Hey, Mr. T. Got a sec?"

Turner glanced around the party. Coach was ensconced in his recliner, some nice painkillers taking off the grumpy edge. His smile was a bit goofy, but he seemed happy to be talking with the twins, Eric and Erica — poor kids, with their matchy names — who were both great in the relay races the season before. Something about that twin sense gave them great instincts for teamwork. Or maybe that was bullshit and it was coincidence. Turner didn't care, so long as they continued cutting the relay teams' overall times down.

Others on the teams, girls and boys, mingled throughout the downstairs. The sofa was lined with kids, but most of them had congregated near the food. Teenagers could decimate a holiday spread like an avalanche taking off trees on the mountainside. Or maybe a plague of locusts was a more apt description.

Eli hadn't returned from the restroom, and Turner's corner of the dining room opposite the table of snacks was relatively quiet for now.

"What's up, Woods?"

Chris shifted nervously. "Well, uh, I heard that you're, um..." He trailed into an undecipherable mumble.

"I didn't catch that?"

"Well, there's that greeting card message out front. 'Make the Yuletide Gay.' And there's some rumors around school about you," Chris said, blushing. "I was just wondering if they're true?"

Turner crossed his arms over his chest, subconsciously puffing up the way he used to when people tried to give Eli shit for being gay. "That's really not a topic for hallway gossip."

Eli returned, having come up behind them. "Good luck with that," he said lightly as he stopped beside Turner. "You'd have been prime gossip material back in my day."

"Yeah, well, I work with these kids. I can't really—"

"Is this your boyfriend?" Chris asked, his face lighting up. "He is, isn't he?"

It was only then that Turner realized how close they stood, with their shoulders touching and their faces close as they murmured to each other.

"Uh," Turner said eloquently to the question.

He hesitated to answer, not because he was afraid of people knowing he was bi. He didn't ordinarily chat about his sexuality with students, but he'd happily claim Eli — if Eli was his for the claiming. He wasn't sure how to define their relationship, except temporary. Could Eli be his boyfriend — a real partner — if only for another couple of weeks?

"I'm Coach's son," Eli said.

Chris looked confused for a second before his gaze flew to Eli's father, and his eyes widened. "You're dating Coach's son? Holy shit," he whispered.

"He's not—" Eli started, but Turner thought *fuck it* and slid an arm around Eli's waist, cutting in.

"I hope we can end up together someday, but Eli's only here for the holidays."

Eli gaped. "You just outed yourself."

"I'm not in," Turner said testily. "I dated Cam Waits, and everyone knows it."

"Whoa, that was true?"

Turner scowled at Chris. "Woods, is there a reason you're so interested in my personal life?"

Chris flushed. "Sorry. I was only asking because we need a sponsor for the GSA meetings at school."

"I thought Lilah Perkins did that?" For Eli's benefit, he added, "She's the director of the local LGBT Center."

"Right, I heard about the center," Eli said. "Things really have changed in Juniper, huh?"

"Some," Turner said. "There's always more that could be done."

"Ms. Perkins quit," Chris said. "And she told us we'd need a new sponsor next week. They're talking about closing down the center."

"Is this more gossip?" Turner asked.

Chris shook his head. "She talked to me because I'm GSA president."

"Oh." That threw Turner. "I didn't realize you were..."

"Pan."

"Excuse me?"

When had they shifted to talking about frying thing? Beside him, Eli laughed. "He means pansexual." At Turner's blank look, Eli elaborated. "It means that you're attracted to someone regardless of their gender."

"Huh." Turner blinked. "And that's different from bisexuality because ..."

"Bi people are attracted to men and women, while gender isn't a factor for pansexuals," Chris said.

Turner tried to wrap his brain around the concept. Was he attracted to men and women, or just people regardless of gender? Maybe he'd had it wrong about himself all along. But ... he did love the soft curves and sweet smells of a woman, and the lean lines and hard cock of a man. So maybe he *was* bi.

"It's just a less binary way to look at sexuality," Eli said.

He certainly knew the lingo. Turner had thought he was enlightened for calling himself bisexual. While he was still trying to figure out pansexual, Eli and Chris started chatting about other sexualities: asexual, graysexual, demisexual, biromantic, aromantic.

"I'm clearly out of my element," Turner told Chris. "Maybe there's someone else you could ask."

Chris's face fell. "There's no other LGBT teachers that I know of, and with the LGBT Center closing, it's looking like we won't have any meeting spaces at all."

"Hey, how come you get to bring a date?" Rachelle said as she walked up, a plate of cookies in one hand.

"That's a load of carbs," Turner said.

She shrugged. "Holiday pass, Mr. T. We'll be you're A-Team when track season starts up."

Eli snorted. "Aren't you a little young to know that show?"

"Aren't you?" she challenged.

"Coach showed them a clip when he brought me on. He thought it'd be hilarious for the kids to call me that. I think he considers Coach a title just for him."

Eli rolled his eyes, probably thinking of his father's ego. But when Turner looked at Coach holding court with the team, he looked more like a man reminiscing about the past than the strong leader he usually was at these parties. It was never easy to let go, but Turner thought Eli might be right. Coach was planning to retire, and for a man like him, who'd immersed most of his life in his job, it wouldn't be easy.

"Back to my point," Rachelle said, looking pointedly at Turner's arm around Eli's waist. "You said we couldn't bring dates. You said you didn't want any shenanigans or canoodling or some other old guy word."

"You're pushing it, Liesen."

"She has a point," Eli said, lips lifting in a playful smile, "if I'm actually your date? Not sure if the Coach's son, who's already invited, can be considered a date. I do live here, after all."

"Half of them are dating each other anyway," Turner pointed out dryly. "They're not really missing out. And, yes, Eli, you're my date. No arguing your way out of it."

Eli grinned. "Why would I want to argue? I've been trying to date you since I was sixteen."

Turner raised his eyebrow. "Just sixteen? I was sure when we were fourteen—"

"Shut up," Eli said with a laugh.

Then Rachelle ruined the moment by continuing to complain. "I'm not dating anyone on the team, though."

"That's what you get for going for the band guy," Chris said.

"Really, Rachelle?" Turner said. "You're dating a guy in a band. That's about as cliché—"

"He doesn't have a band," she interrupted. "He's *in* band. On the trombone."

"Oh."

"Yeah, you know what they say about assuming," she said. "Damon isn't cliché. He's cute and sweet and a great musician."

"A trombonist with a bright future," Eli said, fighting a smile. "Apologize to the girl for being so judgy."

"My deepest apologies," Turner said.

Chris finally got impatient. "What about the GSA?"

"Look, it stands for gay-straight alliance," Turner said. "The sponsor doesn't have to be gay or bi or any of those other letters in the acronyms I clearly don't know."

Chris huffed. "If you don't know, a straight teacher really won't. Besides, most of us would feel more comfortable with someone who understands what it's like to be queer."

Turner cringed. He knew the younger generation used the word, but he'd also heard it flung negatively at Eli. He glanced at his face to see if it bothered him. He stood with a bland smile, but Turner sensed his discomfort with it.

"Let's just say LGBTQ for now."

Chris frowned. "But I'm pan. I'm not in those letters, unless you use Q to mean queer, and then why wouldn't we just say queer? That includes everyone."

Eli nudged Turner. "Queer is acceptable, and if these kids feel comfortable with it, let them choose their own labels, yeah?"

"But..."

"I know," Eli said, his eyes showing that he really did know. "But I'm used to it after working at Rainbow Haven."

"The LGBT youth shelter in California," Turner said. "You must have a lot of experience with young people."

The first tendrils of an idea drifted into his mind.

"Yeah," Eli said. "I mean, I was an event planner and marketing director. I didn't do counseling."

"Neither did Ms. Jenkins," Chris said helpfully. Maybe he'd figured out where Turner was headed. "She just managed the center, coordinated events, and gave us a safe place to meet there and at school."

"Oh. Well, it's a shame you're losing her," Eli said.

"Maybe you could help out?" Rachelle said, chiming in at the perfect moment. Turner was afraid Eli would balk if he pushed him. But coming from the teens ...

Eli shook his head. "I'm sorry. I don't live here."

"Have you gotten any job leads?" Turner asked.

"I haven't tried yet," Eli said. "The holidays aren't really the right time to job hunt."

"Of course," he said agreeably. Eli cast him a suspicious look, and he did his best to appear neutral. He couldn't try to ram the idea down Eli's throat. That would never fly. But if he gently made suggestions, allowing Eli to think them over on his own, maybe Eli would come to see that Juniper could be home again.

God, the thought made hope flutter in his chest. To have Eli permanently. To have a real partner, someone to kiss when he came home from work, someone to tease him over his running addiction and to cuddle Scout when he was busy. Someone to help his mother when he couldn't, and to crawl into bed with him and hold him after a rough day. What would that be like?

I want that. I want it so fucking bad. But is it asking too much?

"Well, I bet the LGBT Center would hire you," Chris offered. "Maybe it wouldn't have to close down."

"Why is it closing?" Eli asked. "Why not just replace her?"

"There's no one else local who's interested. I guess she's been planning to leave for a long time, and they've tried to find a replacement. They don't have the money to do a national search and fly people in, so ..." Chris shrugged. "We're out of luck. We won't even have a GSA unless Mr. T helps."

Eli turned on him, eyes intent. "You have to do it, Turner."

"I'm not very well equipped. I don't know half the new terminology—"

"It doesn't matter. You were my safe place in high school, Turner. You were my personal GSA. You're supportive and a good listener. That's all they need."

"Aw, you guys are totes adorbs," Rachelle said.

Turner shot her a look. "Whole words, Liesen. What have I told you?"

"You told me not to bring a date to the party," she said with sass. "And yet ..."

After that, the conversation devolved into a mock stern

exchange in which Rachelle was threatened with extra laps or even a special practice over the holidays, and Chris and Eli laughed at them both.

It was so amazing to see Eli happy here in Juniper. It felt like it'd been forever since he'd beamed that joy at Turner. It was intoxicating stuff, and he didn't think twice about leaning in to peck a kiss on Eli's cheek.

Eli looked at him, eyes warm, and Turner knew he was toast.

If he and Eli didn't find a way to stay together, he'd be gutted. But it would be a hell of an experience until then, and he had no intention of giving up even a second of the time they had together.

17

Eli leaned against Turner on the sofa, his head cushioned against the fake fur of Turner's open Santa coat and his cheek against warm skin.

"Hot Santa," he murmured, running his hand over Turner's belly. "Furry Santa. Hmm. There's a whole new kink."

Turner's belly quivered under him as he laughed. Apparently, you didn't need a big belly to shake like jelly, as the Santa stories went. Granted, Turner's jelly was nice and firm ... a solid mold.

"Actually, I think Santa is the original Daddy," Turner said.

Eli pulled his hand away with a shudder and started to sit up. "Oh, ugh, now I'm thinking of my father. You do *not* want that if you're planning to get lucky tonight."

After the holiday party wrapped up, Eli and Turner had helped clean up the worst of the mess, then sat at the table and shared a cup of hot chocolate with his mother and father. It had been a surreal experience, as Coach talked about the importance of tradition in sports — a not-so-subtle message that he wanted Turner to carry on his traditions after he left the team? — and his mother spoke about how lovely it was to have Eli home for the holidays. Coach had quietly but sincerely agreed, and Turner had squeezed Eli's knee under the table.

He felt so welcome, so moved by this inclusion he'd thought he'd never feel again, that he hadn't been able to speak around the lump in his throat. He'd gulped his hot chocolate and managed to finally say, "You guys shouldn't say that until after you see the presents I got you. You might be disappointed."

Turner laughed, innately understanding that Eli needed to lighten the moment. His mother had scolded. "Honestly, Eli, as if we care about presents." And his father had smirked. "I don't know, that vibrating massager you got me has gone to good use." He'd winked at Eli's mother, which — *ew* — and she'd thrown a cookie at him. "Don't give him any ideas!"

Gross parental sex images aside, it had been nice.

Turner had offered to load the dishwasher, and Eli's parents had gracefully taken the offer and headed to bed. Eli was relieved to be alone with Turner, even if it meant doing dishes at 11 p.m.

Turner pulled Eli back against him, shifting so he was lying on the sofa with Eli resting on top of him. Eli closed his eyes, absorbing the feel of Turner's body beneath him. The heat of his skin and the itchy tickle of his body hair. The solidness of a body that was firm with muscle, and yet, there was softness to him too.

Eli lay with him, watching the lights on the Christmas tree and lightly petting his fingers over Turner's chest hair. "Don't you need to get home to Scout?"

"Nah. I didn't want to chance it after the chocolate fiasco. I took him to spend the night with Krystal. He was delighted to play with Anthony for an evening."

Turner smoothed a hand down Eli's back. "This is nice. Just being here with you."

"Yeah," Eli murmured, his eyes half closed.

"Wouldn't it be nice if we could have this every night?"

Eli's eyes popped open. He'd tensed automatically, and Turner rubbed his hand on his back. "Shh. I'm not asking you to decide anything now."

"But you will later?" Eli asked with an edge to his voice he couldn't curtail.

Turner sighed. "Eli..."

Eli sat up, putting some distance between them. "I knew when you brought up that LGBT Center job. You want me to move back here. Even though my life is there."

"How is your life there any more than it's here?" Turner asked. "Your life is wherever you choose to live. But you haven't mentioned that many close friends. Your job is gone, and you rent, right? So you could easily move."

"I have friends," he said defensively.

Bosses and roommates counted as friends, right? Barb had stayed in touch since he left, and okay, things weren't great with Levi right now, but it wasn't his fault that Eli lost his job and left town abruptly. Besides, he had friends from college he stayed in touch with via Facebook. They didn't live in California, though, so that didn't really help his case.

"It's my life," Eli added. "I choose how and where I live it."

Turner cupped his face in his hands. "Eli, I know. I'm not telling you to do anything. I'm not even asking. I was thinking out loud. I'm sorry."

Turner kissed him gently. Then again. "I just wish ..."

"Me too," Eli whispered.

As Turner pulled him back down onto the sofa, he didn't tell him that he'd had these thoughts all on his own without Turner's prompting. That he wondered what if ...

What if we could stay together? What if I didn't have to leave? Or what if Turner could come with me?

The thoughts made his heart race and his palms grow sweaty, and they scared him almost too much to examine rationally. Because there were the other what-ifs. What if this was all he ever got with Turner? What if this holiday was their one and only season together?

He tried not to think about the what-ifs and enjoy the right now. So when Turner suggested he should get home, Eli grabbed a few things from his bedroom and went with him. He might be too afraid to talk about their future, but he was going to spend as much time with Turner as possible before the what-ifs became the what-is.

———————

They kissed slowly, thoroughly, as Turner walked Eli to the bed, gripping his hips and guiding him step by step. Eli clung to him, arms around Turner's neck as they moved without breaking their kiss.

Turner always loved kissing Eli. From the lightest brush of lips to the full-fledged assault Eli waged when he was turned on, all of it was good. Tonight, it was different.

Their love-making was bittersweet, as if they were already saying goodbye. Eli's kisses were achingly sweet, slow explorations of his mouth. Each touch lingered as if Eli were trying to memorize the feel of Turner's skin beneath his fingers.

It broke Turner's heart and made him angry by turns because he knew Eli wanted more with him than a holiday fling. And he refused to have some sort of maudlin sex.

He broke the kiss.

"Listen to me, Eli," he said, waiting for Eli to meet his eyes. "This is not the last time we'll be together like this. Not tonight and not on New Year's Eve. When you go back to California, then you go. But you and me? We aren't done."

Eli's breath caught as his eyes searched Turner's face. "But... how?"

"Somehow," Turner said resolutely, though he had no fucking idea. He only knew he wasn't willing to lose Eli again. Did he want him to stay in Juniper? Yes. One hundred percent yes. But would he ask Eli to do that? No. He couldn't. He *wouldn't*.

Maybe they'd maintain a long-distance relationship, visiting each other once a month and on holidays. Fuck the people who said that would doom them to failure. There were phone calls and video chat and texting. Turner could spend an entire summer in California. He could spend spring break and winter break with Eli. They could make it happen.

Or hell, if that didn't work, maybe he'd just leave his job here and go. There would be other coaching jobs. He wasn't so sure about his mother. Maybe he could move her too. Or wait until she didn't need him so much. *Right, because that day's just around the corner.*

"Hey, where did you go?" Eli asked.

Turner breathed out slowly, trying to calm his own anxious heart. "Sorry. Just thinking."

Eli tried to smile. "Let's just be in the moment for now. Everything else can wait."

His eyes told Turner he didn't believe him. Turner pushed Eli down on the bed, then joined him, holding him tight. "Eli, we'll figure it out."

"Okay," Eli said.

"I love you."

There was a beat of silence. Then Eli levered up on an elbow to look down at Turner. "You're not pulling any punches, are you?"

"I'm not asking you for anything."

"Aren't you?" Eli smiled more genuinely. "Maybe you're not. You already know you have my love. Don't you?"

Turner gazed up at him, a smile tugging at his own lips. "I wouldn't want to presume," he said, echoing the line Eli had given him at the bar the night they had drinks with Cam. Damn, but that felt so long ago now.

"Oh, you can presume all you want, Mr. T," Eli teased, before lowering himself over Turner to kiss him. "Presume you can get naked with me. Presume you can fuck me."

Turner hands tightened on Eli's ass. "That's a lot of presuming."

"Mmm-hmm. Presume I want you, Turner. Every inch of you."

Turner kneaded Eli's ass, each cheek fitting perfectly in his palms. Such a tight, perfect little ass that would feel amazing around his dick. So far, he'd only felt Eli's hands and his mouth, and until two seconds ago, he'd been okay with that. Eli's words sparked a fire inside him, though. Now, he was aching to take Eli, to plunge deep into his body, to know the feel of him from the inside out.

"Get naked," he growled. "I'm going to give you exactly what you want."

Eli yanked off his clothes in a hurry, tossing them to the floor without a care. He was desperate to have Turner over him, inside him. Love confessions seemed to be a good aphrodisiac because he was burning up, and Turner had barely touched him.

Turner shoved down his jeans beside him, and Eli spared a moment to admire his cock, before he yanked open Turner's top bedside table drawer. As expected, he found a box of condoms, some lube, and a few sheets with recorded running times. It appeared to be some sort of running diary.

"Really?" Eli said in disbelief. "Do you jerk off to fantasies about jogging down the trail?"

Turner chuckled, leaning in to bite his shoulder as he looked past Eli to the papers in the drawer. "Only if you're running in front of me. That ass of yours." His hand slipped down to caress one bare cheek. "Let's just say that if you hadn't fallen when you went running with me, I probably would have tripped over my own feet while staring at your ass."

Eli snorted. "You're skilled enough to run and leer, but I appreciate the sentiment."

Turner squeezed Eli's ass cheek, then slipped one finger into his crease and slid it down until the pad of his finger brushed over his hole.

Eli grabbed the lube and handed it back. "Make yourself useful back there."

Turner chuckled, kissed Eli's shoulder, and murmured again, "I love you."

"You love my ass, you mean."

"Mmm. I'm going to make love to your ass," Turner agreed. He pumped the lube bottle, getting a good-sized dollop of liquid on his finger, and smeared the cool gel over Eli's hole. Eli shivered, trying not to tense up as Turner circled his fingertip around his rim. Turner's hands were big, his fingers were thick, and Eli now knew from experience that taking his fingers was a stretch all on its own.

Turner pressed his fingertip forward, and Eli exhaled, forcing his body to accept the intrusion.

"Damn, baby, you're tight."

Eli grunted as Turner pushed deeper, then retreated to add more lube and slide in again. "Your fingers are big."

"Not as big as my dick," he breathed into Eli's ear. "And you want my big dick in you, don't you? It's gonna burn, but then it'll feel so good."

Eli's breath quickened, Turner's dirty words doing the trick, which was probably his intention. Eli rocked back on his finger, taking it deeper, and moaned as his cock got so hard and achy it trailed precum on the sheets.

Turner cradled his body from behind, stabilizing Eli where he lay on his side. Even though they weren't face-to-face, it felt incredibly intimate with Turner breathing against his neck. Each time he spoke, he murmured directly into Eli's ear, and Eli could feel Turner's chest pressed against his back. He felt surrounded by Turner's body, held close and embraced in the position.

Turner slid his finger deeper, turning it to seek out Eli's prostate, and Eli purred his pleasure. "Better," he whispered.

"Oh, it's going to get lots better," Turner agreed.

He pulled back, adding more lube, and Eli felt two fingertips prod at his hole before Turner pushed. They went in easier, though not without some pain. Eli took them, his mind already imagining Turner's cock filling him up. He wanted to know that feeling, even if it hurt. Pleasure would be just around the corner. Orgasmic extasy not far beyond that.

"You're trembling," Turner said, his hand going still. "Am I rushing this? I thought ..."

"What?" Eli asked breathlessly.

"I thought you probably bottomed a lot," he said sheepishly. "Not that you're easy or anything. But the way you talked with Cam..." He groaned. "And now I'm talking about my ex while my fingers are in your ass. Smooth."

Eli chuckled. "Wow, and I thought I was wound up. You're nervous."

"I just want this to be perfect," Turner said, dropping a kiss on Eli's neck. "We've waited a long time."

"It's already perfect; we're together," Eli said. "And to answer your implied question, I have bottomed plenty. But not for a while. And you're larger than average. Okay?"

"I see," Turner said with a smug note in his voice.

"Yes, Turner, your cock is big. Now, how about we get to the part where you make me feel it?"

Turner groaned. "Now?"

"Now."

Turner rolled on a condom, slathering it with lube with one hand while he kept two fingers in Eli's ass, scissoring them to spread him just a bit more. Eli said he was ready, but as they'd discussed, Turner's cock was thick. Sometimes that was a blessing, and sometimes when he wanted to fuck a guy, it was a curse.

He didn't know Eli's sexual desires well enough yet to predict which it'd be with him. If it was too much, they could go back to hand jobs and blow jobs, and Turner would still be impossibly happy to have Eli in his bed. In his life at all.

He withdrew his fingers, lined up his cock, and pushed.

Eli hissed, body going tense. But just as Turner froze, worried he was pushing him too fast, Eli shoved back onto his dick, taking half of him deep into his body. Eli's ass squeezed around him painfully, and he groaned. "Jesus, Eli!"

Eli worked his hips forward and back, taking Turner inch by inch. Turner's mind was blown, all his awareness focused on his hard, aching dick. But eventually he came back to himself enough to give a thrust as Eli pushed back and watched as his cock slid into Eli to the hilt. "Fuck."

"Yeah," Eli said in a strained voice.

"Am I hurting you?"

"Just give me a second to adjust."

Turner stroked his hand up Eli's side, then down. He pressed kisses over his shoulders and neck. This served two purposes: to relax Eli and to help Turner focus on something other than the drive to thrust. Gradually, kiss by kiss, tension leaked out of Eli, and his body stopped fighting Turner.

"Now," Eli murmured. "Fuck me."

Turner placed one last kiss on Eli's shoulder, rocked forward, and reveled in the sound of pleasure that broke from Eli's lips. He rocked again, and Eli shifted his hips, moving with him.

"Want to see your face," Eli gasped as Turner thrust in again, a bit harder.

"Yeah, me too," Turner said, carefully pulling out and turning on his back. "Ride me, baby."

Eli straddled his hips, grabbed his cock, and pressed it against his hole. Pressing back, he took Turner in one smooth slide.

"So good," Turner said as Eli impaled himself on his dick. He looked gorgeous sitting there, his chest gleaming with sweat, his face flushed, and his lips ruby red. "Kiss me."

Eli leaned forward to kiss him, and Turner took the opportunity to stroke his hands over every inch of Eli he could reach. His thighs, muscles tense from his squatting position over Turner. His softer flanks, his pebbled nipples. Turner pinched and twisted, drinking down little cries and gasps from Eli.

Finally, Eli pulled back and began to rock up and down, setting a steady rhythm. Turner bent his legs, using his feet and hips to piston his cock up, meeting Eli's downward thrusts. They grunted and groaned together, panting for breath, and their lovemaking gave way to two bodies working on instinct, chasing the pleasure that built between them.

"Turner," Eli gasped. "You feel..."

"I know, baby," Turner said as the feeling crested.

"So close," Eli whimpered.

Turner had an epiphany — *aha, I should ...* — and grabbed Eli's cock, stroking it firmly. Eli came with a broken cry, pumping into his hand, his hole tightening rhythmically around Turner's dick.

Turner stroked him through it, watching in fascination as Eli's cum splattered his chest, and then grabbed Eli's waist and held him in place as he thrust into his sated body three more times and came hard.

Eli slid off Turner, turning into a boneless puddle and landing on the sheets beside him. "Not bad," he muttered. "Seven out of ten."

"*Seven?*"

Eli laughed breathlessly. "Don't feel bad. I've had so many California men—"

He didn't get to finish that statement, shouting in surprise as Turner jabbed him in the ribs, then yanked him under his body and kissed him hard. "Tell me I'm the best you've ever had," Turner ordered.

Eli grinned up at him. He probably looked goofy. He was still sweaty and sticky with his own cum, and his ass throbbed with the echo of that large cock inside him. And despite having no idea what their future held — if they even had a future — he was blissed out with a post-orgasmic high. "You're the best," he confirmed.

Turner kissed him again, more gently. "You too," he said.

Eli idly wondered what sex was like with women for Turner. Much the same, but without the gymnastics of dealing with a tight ass? He probably didn't have to spend ten minutes waiting for some chick to handle his dick.

"The best man," Eli said. "Right? It must be different with women."

"It's different," Turner agreed. Then he swatted Eli's ass. "You're still the best of anyone. Man or woman."

"Yeah?"

"Oh, yeah." Turner kissed him again. "I can't get enough of you, Eli Harp."

Eli smiled. "The feeling's mutual."

18

December 25th

E li woke up Christmas morning in his childhood bedroom. Alone.

He didn't much like it. He'd gotten used to the heat of Turner warming his back. Even when Turner wasn't blanketing his body with sweaty skin and hair, the man put off enough heat to give Eli a cozy, comforting warmth as he woke. Not to mention the warmth he evoked in Eli's chest simply by smiling at him.

He was gone over Turner, and he knew it. They'd spent every minute together since the school session went on break. Eli hadn't even bothered to sneak around, letting his mom know that he'd be at Turner's place for the rest of the holiday vacation. He figured she could tell Coach, even if that was a bit cowardly of him.

She'd hugged him, told him it was a long time coming, and waved him off with a smile.

It had been great: having sex late into the night, sleeping in, waking up to exchange sleepy hand jobs or blow jobs, going out for brunch. Afterward, he'd pop over to check on his parents while Turner went running — crazy man that he was — and to check in on his family. They'd take care of any errands they had, then meet up for dinner and do it all over again.

*I don't want it to en*d, Eli thought. *I really don't think I could take it.*

Eli had tentatively put out some feelers about the LGBT Center job, but he hadn't heard anything, it being the holidays. In a way, he was convinced it would be too easy. Jobs didn't fall into your lap at the perfect time so you could have a happy ending. But the least he could do was try. There were other jobs in Juniper — and if he couldn't find one in town, he could most likely find something in Portland. At least he'd be in the same state. It would make weekend visits easier to accomplish.

Eli showered and dressed in a pair of dark jeans and a white dress shirt under a crimson sweater. It was a little preppy, but it was Christmas Day, and he wasn't sure who would be in the house when he ventured out.

His mom was in the kitchen at the stove. "Honestly, Mom, you've done enough cooking to last a lifetime. You should relax."

She smiled at him. "I don't mind. You're looking handsome today."

Eli brushed at his sweater self-consciously. "Too much?"

He didn't really know how Christmas went at his parents' place now that they'd included Turner's family. He felt a little like an outsider.

"No, it's good. I half expected you to be at Turner's place."

Eli frowned. "I came home for a family Christmas. I wouldn't blow that off."

"I know you wouldn't. But it would have been okay to wait and come over with him, sweetie. You've been so happy this past week."

"What about you?" Eli asked, concerned by his mother's dedication to the kitchen. Was she hiding out there because she loved it, as Coach said, or was there more to it? "Are you happy?"

"Of course I am," she said.

"Mom, I know you like baking and all, but surely there's something more you want out of life?"

She shook her head. "Honestly, Eli, do you think this is all I do? Of course it's not. I always bake more over the holidays. It's fun hosting family and friends. But the rest of the year, especially without you around?" She laughed. "I make Coach fend for himself half the time."

"Oh."

She leaned in. "You want to know a secret?"

"Sure."

"I started writing for fun. Fan fiction." She blushed. "I found it after I got a computer to keep up with you on Facebook. I even write M/M pairings. That means male/male."

"I kind of figured," Eli said, realizing he didn't know his mother as well as he'd thought. But if she wrote, that explained where he came by his word skills. It certainly hadn't come from Coach. And it was kind of encouraging she was writing male couples. She'd always said she accepted Eli, but this reassured him that she didn't have any reservations she was hiding away.

"Well, anyway, it's just a bit of fun," she said. "But I have some fans."

"No kidding," Eli said with a grin. "That's really great."

She shrugged a shoulder. "It's just a hobby, but who knows? Maybe I'll publish something one day. In the meantime, I'm glad you came home, and I'm happy to cook up a storm. Don't you worry!"

Eli smiled at her enthusiasm. "I'm glad I came home too."

"It's nice to see you and Turner patch things up. It was so sad to see you two driven apart."

Eli swallowed, joining her at the counter. She ladled a dollop of batter into the pan for another pancake. She'd piled a few on a plate already.

"Yeah. Turner and I are friends again."

"And more?" she asked.

Eli hesitated. Of course, they were more. Turner had even said he loved Eli, and he felt the same. But they hadn't figured out their future yet. Eli had ideas about that, but he and Turner needed to talk more.

"We're working on it," he said finally.

"Well, I'm happy for you," she said. "I hope it all works out as it should." She smiled. "You tell Turner that I'll look after Daisy, if it comes down to it. You two need to live your life for yourselves, not your parents."

Wow. His mom *really* wanted him and Turner to be together. He knew Turner didn't only help out his own mom, but Eli's parents as well. He smiled. "Thanks, Mom. I don't think it'll come to that."

"Well, still," she said.

He nodded toward the stove. "Need help with anything?"

"Set the table and pour coffee and juice? The Williamses will be over any minute now."

"Sure," he said, happy to have a task to occupy his nervous hands.

Today, he'd tell Turner what he really wanted for Christmas: a future together. Whatever it took.

When Turner and his family arrived at the Harps' home, they had breakfast and then gathered in the living room to dig into Christmas stockings. Anthony crawled under the tree and began handing out presents. Everything was happening at once, a sort of organized chaos, but Turner was content to watch Eli's expressions. Anthony was buzzing with excitement, and every time Eli looked in his direction, he smiled as if the kid's joy was contagious. Which maybe it was.

A present was thrust into Turner's hands. He glanced at the

tag, noticed it said it was from Eli, and eagerly tore away the wrapping. When he found the dartboard, along with a keychain convertible, he laughed out loud.

"You're such a brat," he said.

Eli was sitting next to him on the couch, trying to go through his stocking while a pile of presents grew at his feet. He smiled tentatively. "Sorry. I bought that the day after the dart incident, and I wanted to make sure you remembered me when I was gone."

Turner's smile faded, and Eli hurried on. "Now, I know you'll remember me. Because ..." He trailed off uncertainly. "You okay?"

No, Turner was not okay. He couldn't go another day with the kind of uncertainty they had. He stood suddenly, grabbing Eli's hand and pulling him up too. "We'll be right back," he announced to the room, where Krystal and Coach had looked over at them curiously.

Keeping a tight grip on Eli's hand, he led him back to his bedroom, where they could speak privately.

"Uh, Turner, it's not really the right time to christen my bedroom," Eli joked nervously.

Turner pulled him inside and closed the door. "Eli, I can't take this—"

"Oh." El tried to take a step back, and Turner tightened his grip on his hand.

"I need to end the uncertainty. I want to be with you. Permanently."

Eli swallowed. "*Oh.* Well, I want to be with you too. You know that."

"I do." Turner took a deep breath. "That's why when you go back to California, I'm going to go with you."

Eli gaped at him, mouth hanging open unattractively. "*Wait, what?*"

Turner repeated himself patiently. "When you leave, I'll go with you. I don't want to figure things out. I want to be with you, officially. It's all I want for Christmas, though the dartboard and car keychain were nice touches."

He smiled as Eli stared. "Say something," he urged. "Tell me that you want to make a life with me too."

Eli bit his lip, a sure sign he was nervous, and Turner's heart twisted in response.

"The thing is, you can't leave your family," Eli said. "I see how much they rely on you. Mine too, actually."

Turner frowned. Was Eli actually saying Turner couldn't leave because he was responsible for *Eli's* family?

Eli shook his head. "I'm saying this wrong. Stop looking so horrified. I want to stay here in Juniper."

Turner blinked. "You do?"

"I've done a lot of thinking the past few days. Bremer, California, wasn't a hot spot of liberal activity either. I dealt with bigots. I met kids who were kicked out of their homes. I chose to live there because I loved working somewhere I could make a difference. And yeah, some of that was driven by my experience as a teen. Coach didn't kick me out, but I always felt like he wanted me gone."

Eli continued. "My memories were so colored by these few events that I forgot that Juniper wasn't all bad. It has good people, too. I've reconnected with Janine. I've met Cam. My family's here. And then there's you. You're all I've ever wanted, Turner."

Turner felt torn. Eli was saying everything he'd hoped to hear, and yet, he was so afraid of letting Eli make the wrong choice. He wanted him happy, above all else. "Are you sure you can handle moving back here?"

"I'm sure."

"And if you don't find a job you like or you're unhappy for any reason, you'll tell me? I don't want you to settle, Eli, even for me. If you're not happy, we'll figure something else out. I don't care, as long as we're together."

"I promise," Eli said. "You offering to move for me, that makes it easier. It feels more like a choice now. This is the choice I think is right for both of us."

Turner pulled him into a hug, hardly daring to believe his words. Eli was going to stay. With Turner. They could be a real, committed couple.

"I love you so much," he murmured into Eli's hair. "Thank you."

"Don't thank me," Eli said, pulling back. "I want to show you something."

Eli turned to the dresser, tugging it out from the wall, then crouched down, pointing to a carving.

E+T inside a heart.

Turner ran the pad of his thumb over it.

"I did that when I was twelve," Eli said.

Turner's eyebrows flew up. "That young?"

"Yeah," Eli said, standing up. "So you see, Turner. There's no need to thank me for staying here. You're all I ever wanted for Christmas."

He kissed him gently. "And now that I have you, I don't plan on giving you up."

EPILOGUE

Two years later

"Look, mistletoe."

Turner pointed up, and Eli's gaze slipped up to see the leaves and berries over their heads in his childhood bedroom doorway. Smiling, he looked back to Turner, prepared for a kiss. But Turner had lowered himself to one knee, a wedding ring in his hand.

Eli raised his hands to his mouth. *Was he ...*

"Eli Harp, I have a question for you. And I'm really nervous. Maybe just as nervous as you were the last time you put mistletoe up in this doorway and kissed me."

There was a murmur behind him, and Eli looked over his shoulder to see his family gathered at the end of the hall, smiling. Even Coach.

"I hope it ends better this time," Eli said faintly.

Turner smiled nervously. "Me too. Because that night, I made a huge mistake. I lost you. For eight long years, I thought I'd missed my chance to love you the way I knew I could."

Eli's eyes burned. Despite the past two years, in which Eli had found so much happiness it almost made the years they'd missed negligible, the old pain bubbled up. They'd come so close to never having one another. Because of Turner's fear of coming out, but also because of Eli's injured pride. He could have kept Turner's friendship, and perhaps they'd have found their way together sooner.

But better late than never, right?

"I would have proposed to you two years ago, and I thought about it last year," Turner admitted, "but I wanted to make sure you were really happy here. You are, aren't you?"

Eli nodded as his eyes blurred with tears he blinked back. He hadn't magically walked into a full-time job with the LGBT Center. They'd offered him part-time hours, and he'd taken them — both so he could stay in Juniper and so the center could stay open. He'd picked up part-time marketing work at the community center and worked two jobs until the LGBT Center won a grant and offered him a full-time position.

He still lived at the mercy of nonprofit fundraising, but he was okay with that. If the job fell through, he'd find something else.

Since he'd returned to Juniper, he'd built a life that included his family and truly accepting friends. He'd even forgiven Desiree for being a beauty that had once dated Turner, and they'd had a few double dates with her and the new yoga instructor boyfriend.

Turner's mom was still a little fragile. Eli didn't think she'd ever really be as independent as she was before her husband died, but she saw her doctors when necessary, and Eli really liked her. They went shopping together, sometimes even with Janine, and they had fun. Turner no longer had the world on his shoulders; Eli did what he could to help with the burden.

"I've never been happier," Eli said honestly and heard someone sob from down the hall. Probably his mother. She'd been overcome with tears when they'd told her Eli was staying in Juniper. Coach had taken it surprisingly well. Even though he was still mystified by homosexuality, he'd hugged Eli on Christmas

Day two years ago and said, "You chose a good man to have at your side."

Turner cleared his throat, held up the ring, and looked at Eli from dark, intense eyes. "Then, Eli Harp, will you marry me?"

"I don't know if you know this, Turner, but this isn't really how mistletoe works."

Eli took pity at the chagrinned look on Turner's face. "But yes! I'll marry you. Of course."

Turner lunged up from his knees, kissing Eli hard, and then slid the ring onto his finger. "That's not how mistletoe works," he grumbled. "I ought to take this back."

"You wouldn't, would you?"

"Not ever," he promised, kissing Eli again. "I love you. I only wish I'd been brave enough to tell you sooner."

"That's okay. You have the rest of your life to make it up to me."

THE END

THANK YOU FOR READING!

Thank you for reading *All I Want Is You*. I'd be so thankful if you could leave a review; even just a few words help!

I offer monthly giveaways in my newsletter, bonus content and more: http://www.tinyurl.com/djandcompany

I also encourage you to join my FB group for fun teasers and other extras: DJ and Company.

You can connect with me on social media in other ways, as well!

Queer Romance Freebie Fan Club Group on Facebook

facebook.com/AuthorDJJamison

twitter.com/DJ_Jamison_

bookbub.com/authors/dj-jamison

goodreads.com/DJ_Jamison

ABOUT THE AUTHOR

DJ Jamison is the author of more than a dozen m/m romances, including the Ashe Sentinel series and the Hearts and Health series. She writes a variety of queer characters, from gay to bisexual to asexual, with a focus on telling love stories that are more about common ground than lust at first sight. DJ grew up in the Midwest in a working-class family, and those influences can be found in her writing through characters coping with real-life problems: money troubles, workplace drama, family conflicts and, of course, falling in love. DJ spent more than a decade in the newspaper industry before chasing her first dream to write fiction. She spent a lifetime reading before that and continues to avidly devour her fellow authors' books each night. She lives in Kansas with her husband, two sons, two fish, one snake, and a sadistic cat named Birdie.

BOOKS BY DJ JAMISON

Ashe Sentinel Connections

Changing Focus

Source of Protection

Rewriting His Love Life

Winter Blom

Hard Press

Chance for Christmas

Hearts and Health

Heart Trouble

Bedside Manner

Urgent Care

Room for Recovery

Surprise Delivery

Orderly Affair

Operation Makeover

My Anti-Series

My Anti-Valentine

My Anti-Boyfriend

My Anti-Marriage

Real Estate Relations

Full Disclosure

Buyer's Remorse

Printed in Great Britain
by Amazon